MAIGRET and the CALAME REPORT

MAIGRET and the CALAME REPORT

Georges Simenon

Translated by Moura Budberg

A Harvest Book
A Helen and Kurt Wolff Book
Harcourt Brace & Company
San Diego New York London

Library of Congress Cataloging-in-Publication Data
Simenon, Georges, 1903–1989
Maigret and the Calame report.
"A Helen and Kurt Wolff book."
Translation of: Maigret chez le ministre.
I. Title.
PQ2637.I53M25613 1987 843'.912 86-31793
ISBN 0-15-655153-5 (Harvest pbk.)

Printed in the United States of America
First Harvest edition 1987
F E D C B

MAIGRET
and the
CALAME REPORT

1

Every evening when he came home Maigret stopped at the same spot on the sidewalk, just after the gas lamp, and raised his eyes to the lighted windows of his apartment. It was an automatic movement. Probably if he had been asked whether there were lights there or not, he would have hesitated before replying. In the same way, almost as if it were a sort of compulsion, he began unbuttoning his coat between the second and the third floor and searching for the key in the pocket of his trousers, though invariably the door opened as soon as he stepped on the door mat.

These were rites that had taken years to become established and to which he was more accustomed than he would have cared to admit to himself. It was not raining tonight, so it did not apply, but his wife, for instance, had a special way of taking his wet umbrella from his hand at the same time as she bent her head to kiss him on the cheek.

He brought out the traditional question:

"No telephone calls?"

She replied, closing the door:

"Yes, there was one. I'm afraid it's hardly worth your while taking off your coat."

The day had been gray, neither hot nor cold, with a sudden shower toward two o'clock in the afternoon. At the Quai des Orfèvres, Maigret had attended only to routine business.

"Did you have a good dinner?"

The light in their apartment was warmer, more intimate than at the office. He could see the newspapers and his slippers waiting for him beside his armchair.

"I had dinner with the boss and Lucas and Janvier at the Brasserie Dauphine."

Afterward the four of them had gone to a meeting of the Police Benevolent Association of which, for three years running and much against his will, Maigret had been elected Vice-President.

"You've got time for a cup of coffee. Take your coat off for a minute. I said you wouldn't be back before eleven."

It was half past ten. The meeting had not lasted long. There had been time for some of them to have a beer in a bar, and Maigret had come home by subway.

"Who called?"

"A Cabinet Minister."

Standing in the middle of the sitting room, he frowned at her.

"What Cabinet Minister?"

"The Minister of Public Works. Point, I think he said."

"That's right, Auguste Point. He telephoned here? Himself?"

"Yes."

"You didn't tell him to call the Quai des Orfèvres?"

"He wanted to speak to you personally. He has to see you very urgently. When I said you weren't in, he wanted to know if I was the maid. He sounded upset. I told him I was Madame Maigret. He apologized, he wanted to know where you were and when you would be back. He sounded timid."

"That's not his reputation."

"He even wanted to know if I was alone or not. And then he explained that his call was to be kept secret, that he wasn't calling from the Ministry but from a public booth and that it was important for him to be in touch with you as quickly as possible."

While she was speaking, Maigret watched her, still frowning, with a look that proclaimed his distrust of politics. It had happened several times during his career that he had been approached by a statesman, a deputy or senator or some high official, but it had always been through the proper channels. He would be summoned to the boss's office and the conversation would always begin with: "I'm sorry, my dear Maigret, to put you in charge of a business you won't like." And it always turned out to be something unsavory.

He was not personally acquainted with Auguste Point; he had never even seen him. Nor was the Minister much quoted in the newspapers.

"Why didn't he call up the Quai?"

He was really talking to himself. But Madame Maigret replied:

"How do I know? I'm only repeating what he said to me. First of all, that he was speaking from a public booth. . . ."

This detail had particularly impressed Madame Maigret, to whom a Cabinet Minister was an individual of some importance, not to be imagined creeping in the dark into a public telephone booth at a street corner.

"He also said that you were not to go to the Ministry, but to his private apartment . . ."

She consulted a scrap of paper on which she had made some notes:

". . . at 27, Boulevard Pasteur. You don't need to waken the concierge, it's on the fourth floor, on the left."

"He's waiting there for me?"

"He'll wait as long as he can. He has to be back at the Ministry before midnight."

Then, in a different tone, she asked:

"Do you think it's a hoax?"

He shook his head, denying the possibility. It was certainly unusual, bizarre, but it did not sound like a hoax.

"Will you have some coffee?"

"No thanks, not after the beer."

Still standing, he poured himself a drop of plum brandy, took a fresh pipe from the mantelpiece, and moved toward the door.

"Good-by."

Back in Boulevard Richard-Lenoir, the humidity that had permeated the air all day had changed to a gray fog that threw a halo around the street lamps. He did not take a taxi, for it was as quick to reach Boulevard Pasteur by subway; besides, he did not feel he was on official business.

All the way, as he stared abstractedly at the gentleman with whiskers reading the newspaper opposite him, he was wondering what it could possibly be that Auguste Point wanted of him and why he had arranged for them to meet so urgently and so mysteriously.

All he knew of Auguste Point was that he was a lawyer from the Vendée—as well as he could remember, from La Roche-sur-Yon—and that he had entered politics late in life. He was one of those deputies elected after the war for their personal qualities and their conduct during the occupation.

Exactly what that conduct had been Maigret did not know. Yet, while others of his colleagues had come and gone and left no trace behind them, Auguste Point had been re-elected time after time, and three months ago, when the last Cabinet was formed, he had been put at the head of the Ministry of Public Works.

The Superintendent had heard no scandal about him of the kind that attached to the majority of public figures. Nor was there any gossip about his wife or his children, if he had any.

By the time he left the subway at the Boulevard Pasteur station, the fog had grown thick and yellow and Maigret could taste its smoky flavor on his lips. He saw no one on the boulevard and heard some steps only in the distance, toward Montparnasse, and a train that whistled as it left the station, going in the same direction.

A few windows were still lighted and gave an impression of peace and security in the darkness. These houses, neither rich nor poor, neither old nor new, and divided into apartments all very much alike, were inhabited mainly by middle-class people, teachers, civil servants, junior executives who took the subway or the bus to work at precisely the same time every morning.

He pressed the entrance door button and, when the door opened, muttered an indistinguishable name (for the benefit of the concierge) as he moved toward the elevator. It was a very narrow elevator, designed for two. Smoothly and noiselessly, it began its slow ascent in a dimly lit stair well. The doors on all floors were of an identical dark brown; even the door mats were alike.

He rang the bell on the left, and the door opened immediately as if someone had been waiting inside with his hand on the knob.

Auguste Point stepped outside and sent the elevator back, as Maigret had forgotten to do it.

"I'm sorry for disturbing you at such a late hour," he murmured. "Will you come in, please?"

Madame Maigret would have been disappointed, for he did not at all correspond to her idea of a Cabinet Minister. He was about the same build and height as the Superintendent, though squarer and heavier-looking, true peasant stock as it were. His roughly chiseled features, the large nose and mouth, put one in mind of a carving in chestnut wood.

He wore a plain gray suit with a nondescript tie. Three things were striking: the thick eyebrows, the size of his mustache, and the long hairs that covered his hands.

He was studying Maigret, without attempting to conceal it, without even a polite smile.

"Sit down, Superintendent."

The apartment, smaller than Maigret's on Boulevard Richard-Lenoir, probably consisted of only two, perhaps three, rooms and the tiniest of kitchens. They had moved from the hall, where some clothes were hanging, to the study, which was typical of a bachelor's quarters. A few pipes hung in a rack on the wall, ten or twelve of them, some of clay, one a beauty of a meerschaum. An old-fashioned desk, like the one Maigret's father had had long ago, was covered with papers and tobacco ash; it had a set of pigeonholes and small drawers. Maigret did not quite dare to examine the photographs on the wall of Auguste Point's father and mother in the same black and gold frames which he might have found in any farm in the Vendée.

Sitting in his swivel chair, so similar to that of Maigret's father, Auguste Point was playing with a box of cigars.

"Would you like . . ." he began.

The Superintendent said, smiling:

"I prefer my pipe."

"Some of this?"

The Minister offered him an open package of gray tobacco and relit his own pipe, which had gone out.

"You must have been surprised when your wife told you . . ."

He was trying to open the conversation but was not pleased with his attempt. Something curious was taking place.

They sat there in the warm, peaceful study, both of the same build and of about the same age, quite openly studying one another. It was as if they had discovered the resemblance and were intrigued by it but were not quite ready yet to admit its existence.

"Look, Maigret, between men like us, there's no point in the usual formalities. I only know you from the newspapers and from what I've heard about you."

"Same with me, Your Excellency."

With a slight gesture, Auguste Point gave Maigret to understand that at this moment the use of the appellation was inappropriate.

"I'm in terrible trouble. Nobody knows it yet, nobody even suspects it, neither the President of the State Council nor even my wife, and she usually knows my every movement. You're the only one I've turned to."

For a moment he looked away and pulled at his pipe, as if embarrassed by what could be mistaken for vulgar flattery.

"I didn't want to do the conventional thing and go straight to the police. What I'm doing is irregular. You were under no obligation to come here, just as you are under no obligation to help me." He got up, with a sigh.

"Will you have a drink?"

And with what could be taken as a smile:

"Don't worry. I'm not trying to bribe you. It's just that tonight I really need a drink myself."

He went into the next room and came back with a half-finished bottle and two thick glasses of the kind used in country inns.

"It's only some homemade spirits that my father distills every autumn. This is about twenty years old."

They looked at each other, each holding a glass.

"Your health!"

"And yours, Your Excellency."

This time Auguste Point seemed not to hear the last words.

"If I don't know how to begin, it isn't because you embarrass me, but because the story is difficult to tell with any degree of clarity. Do you read the newspapers?"

"I do, on the nights when the criminals allow me some peace."

"You follow political events?"

"Not much."

"You know that I'm not what is called a politician?"

Maigret nodded in affirmation.

"Very well. You're probably aware of the Clairfond disaster?"

This time Maigret could not help giving a start, and a certain anxiety, a certain caution, must have shown in his face, since the other man bent his head and added in a low voice:

"Unhappily, this is what it's all about!"

A short time ago in the subway, Maigret had tried to puzzle out why the Minister had arranged to meet him in secret. The Clairfond affair had never entered his mind, though recently all the newspapers had been full of it.

The Sanatorium of Clairfond, in Haute-Savoie, between Ugines and Mégève, at an elevation of 4,500 feet, was one of the most spectactular postwar achievements. It had been built some years ago, and Maigret had no idea who was originally responsible for the idea of establishing a place for abandoned children comparable to modern privately run sanatoria. At the time it had been much in the news. Some people had seen in it a purely political maneuver and there had been violent debates in the Chamber of Deputies. A commission had been selected to study the project and eventually, after much discussion, it had been realized.

A month later came the disaster, one of the most distressing in history. Snow had begun to melt at a time when no human memory could recall its happening before. The mountain streams had swelled, as did a subterranean river, the Lize, of so little importance that it is not even marked on the map. It had undermined the foundations of a whole wing at Clairfond.

The inquiry, opened on the day after the disaster, had not yet been completed. The experts could not come to an agreement. Neither could the newspapers which, according to their political persuasion, defended different theses.

One hundred and twenty-eight children had died as one of the buildings had collapsed completely; the others were urgently evacuated.

After a moment of silence Maigret murmured:

"You were not in the Cabinet at the time of the construction, were you?"

"No. I wasn't even a member of the parliamentary commission that allocated the funds. To tell you the truth, up to a day or so ago I only knew what everyone knows of the business from the newspapers."

He paused.

"Have you heard anything about the Calame report, Superintendent?"

Maigret glanced at him, surprised, and shook his head.

"You will be hearing about it soon. I'm afraid you'll be hearing too much about it. I suppose you don't read the weekly papers, the *Rumor,* for instance?"

"Never."

"Do you know Hector Tabard?"

"By name and reputation only. My colleagues of the Rue des Saussaies would know him better than I do."

He was referring to the Criminal Investigation Department, which came under the Ministry of the Interior and was often asked to deal with cases of political connotation.

Tabard was a carping journalist whose gossip-filled weekly had the reputation of a cheap blackmailing sheet.

"Read this—it appeared six days after the disaster."

It was short, mysterious.

"Will someone decide one day, under pressure of public opinion, to reveal the contents of the Calame report?"

"Is that all?" The Superintendent was surprised.

"Here is another item:

" 'Contrary to popular belief, it will not be because of foreign policy, nor because of events in North Africa, that the present government will fall at the end of the spring, but because of the Calame report. Who is withholding the Calame report?' "

There was an almost comic sound to the words and Maigret smiled as he asked:

"Who is Calame?"

But Auguste Point was not smiling. He emptied his pipe into a large copper ashtray while he explained:

"He was a professor of the National School of Civil Engineering. He died two years ago, of cancer, I believe. His name is not widely known, but it is famous in the world of engineering and public works. Calame was called in as consultant for large projects in countries as different as Japan and South America, and he was an indisputable authority on everything concerning the resistance of building material, particularly concrete. He wrote a book, which neither you nor I have read, but which every architect knows, called *The Diseases of Concrete.*"

"Was Calame involved in the building of Clairfond?"

"Only indirectly. Let me tell you the story in a different way, more from my own standpoint. At the time of the disaster, as I told you, I knew nothing of the sanatorium that was not in the newspapers. I couldn't even remember whether I had voted for or against the project five years earlier. I had to look up the records to find out that I had voted for it. Like you, I don't read the *Rumor*. It was only after the second item appeared that the President of the Council called me in and asked me: 'Do you know the Calame report?'

"I replied candidly that I did not. He seemed surprised, and I'm not sure that he didn't glance at me with a certain suspicion.

" 'It should be among your archives,' he said to me.

"It was then that he told me the whole story. During the debate on the subject of Clairfond, five years ago, as the parliamentary commission was divided, one of the deputies, I don't know who, had suggested consulting the opinion of an engineer of unquestioned standing. He proposed Professor Julien Calame, of the National School of Civil Engineering, and the latter spent some time studying the project and even investigated the site in Haute-Savoie. He then made a report which normally should have been transmitted to the commission."

Maigret began to understand.

"This report was unfavorable?"

"Wait! When the President talked to me about it, he had already ordered a search in the archives of the Chamber of Deputies. The report should have been in the files of the commission. It turned out that not only was it not there, but that part of the minutes had also disappeared. You see what it all means?"

"That there were people interested in keeping the report unpublished?"

"Read this."

It was another item from the *Rumor*, again short, but no less menacing.

"Is Monsieur Arthur Nicoud powerful enough to prevent the Calame report from seeing the light of day?"

Maigret knew that name as he knew hundreds of others. He had heard of the firm Nicoud and Sauvegrain because it was mentioned almost everywhere where there were public works, whether roads, bridges, or dams.

"It was the firm of Nicoud and Sauvegrain that built Clairfond."

Maigret was beginning to regret that he had come. Though he was drawn spontaneously to Auguste Point, what the man was telling him made him as uneasy as when he had to listen to dirty stories in the presence of a woman.

He could not help wondering what part Auguste Point

could have played in the tragedy that had cost the lives of a hundred and twenty-eight children. He was almost on the brink of asking brusquely:

"And where do you come into all this?"

He could imagine that some people had taken bribes, politicians, perhaps persons in high office.

"I'll try to finish quickly. The President, as I said, asked me to organize a thorough search in the archives of my Ministry. The National School of Civil Engineering comes under the Ministry of Public Works, so that, logically, we should have had at least a copy of the Calame report somewhere in our files."

The words "Calame report" sounded more ominous each time they were repeated.

"You found nothing?"

"Nothing. We searched through tons of paper among files in the attic, and we found nothing."

Maigret was beginning to feel restless, ill at ease in his chair, and the other man noticed it.

"You don't like politics?"

"That's correct."

"Neither do I. Strange as it may seem, it was to fight against politics that twelve years ago I agreed to run for office. And when, three months ago, I was asked to join the Cabinet, it was again the thought of bringing some cleanliness into public affairs that made me do it. My wife and I are simple people. You can see the sort of apartment we stay at in Paris, during the parliamentary sessions, since I have become a deputy. It is more like a bachelor's place. My wife could have remained in La Roche-sur-Yon, where we have a house, but we are not in the habit of living apart."

He was speaking quite naturally, without any hint of sentimentality in his voice.

"Since I have become a Minister, we live officially in the Ministry, Boulevard Saint-Germain, but we come here for some privacy as often as we can, particularly on Sundays. But all that is beside the point. If I called you from a public booth, as your wife no doubt told you—for if I'm not mistaken you have the same kind of wife as I have—it's because I'm suspicious of being overheard. I'm convinced, rightly or wrongly, that all my calls from the Ministry, maybe even from here, are recorded somewhere, I prefer not to know where. I might add, to my shame, that this evening I walked in one door of a movie theater on the boulevard and out of the other and twice changed taxis. I can't even be sure this house is not being watched."

"I saw no one as I arrived."

Maigret was beginning to feel sorry for Auguste Point. Up to now the latter had tried to talk with calm and detachment. But when he came to the essential point of their meeting, he began to hesitate, to go around in circles, as though he feared that Maigret would get a false impression of him.

"The Ministry's archives have been turned upside down, and God alone knows how many papers are kept there of which no human being has any memory. During this time I had telephone calls from the President at least twice a day, and I'm not at all sure that he trusts me. Searches have been made also in the School of Civil Engineering without any result until yesterday morning."

Maigret couldn't help asking, as one does at the end of a novel:

"The Calame report has been found?"

"Something, anyway, that appears to be the Calame report."

"Where?"

"In the attic of the school."

"A professor?"

"A supervisor. Yesterday morning I was given a note with the name of Piquemal on it, of whom I'd never heard. Someone had marked it in pencil: 'With reference to the Calame report.' I ordered him in at once. I dismissed my secretary, Mademoiselle Blanche, from the room, though she's been with me for twenty years, as she comes from La Roche-sur-Yon and worked in my office there. You'll see that this has some bearing on the matter. My parliamentary private secretary was not in the room either. I was left alone with a man of middle age who stood staring at me, saying nothing, with a gray paper parcel under his arm.

" 'Monsieur Piquemal?' I asked, a little anxiously, because for a moment I thought that I was facing a maniac.

"He nodded.

" 'Sit down.'

" 'It's not worth while.'

"I had the impression that his eyes weren't friendly. He asked me, almost impertinently:

" 'Are you the Minister?'

" 'Yes.'

" 'I'm a supervisor at the School of Civil Engineering.'

"He stepped forward, handed me the parcel, and uttered in the same tone:

" 'Open it and give me a receipt.'

"The parcel contained a document of about forty pages, obviously a carbon copy, and headed:

" 'Report concerning the construction of a sanatorrium at Clairfond in Haute-Savoie.' The document was not signed by hand, but the name of Julien Calame with his titles was typed at the bottom of the page, as well as the date.

"Still standing, Piquemal repeated:

" 'I want a receipt.'

"I wrote one out for him. He folded it, slipped it into a worn brief case, and moved to the door. I called him back.

" 'Where did you find these papers?'

" 'In the attic.'

" 'You will probably be called upon to make a written declaration.'

" 'You know where to find me.'

" 'Have you shown this document to anyone else?'

"He looked me straight in the eyes, with contempt.

" 'To no one.'

" 'There were no other copies?'

" 'Not so far as I know.'

" 'Thank you.' "

Auguste Point looked at Maigret in embarrassment.

"That is where I made a mistake," he went on. "I think it was because of Piquemal's strange behavior, for he looked like an anarchist about to throw his bomb."

"How old was he?" asked Maigret.

"Forty-five, perhaps. Neither well dressed nor badly dressed. His eyes were the eyes of a fanatic or a madman."

"Did you get any information about him?"

"Not right away. It was five o'clock. There were still four or five people in my waiting room, and I had to preside at an engineers' dinner in the evening. When my visitor left, my secretary came in and I slipped the Calame report into my personal brief case. I should have telephoned the President of the Council. If I didn't do so, I swear to you that it was again because I was wondering if Piquemal were mad. There was nothing to prove that the document wasn't a forgery. Almost every day we are visited by some demented creature or other."

"Same with us."

"In that case you can understand me. My appointments lasted until seven o'clock. I just had time to go to my apartment and change."

"Did you talk to your wife about it?"

"No. I took my brief case with me. I told her I'd come to Boulevard Pasteur after dinner. This kind of thing often happens. Not only do we meet here on Sunday for a little meal that she cooks, but I also come here alone when I have something important to do and want peace and quiet."

"Where was the banquet?"

"At the Palais d'Orsay."

"You took your brief case with you?"

"It remained, under lock and key, in the care of my driver, in whom I have complete confidence."

"You came back here directly after?"

"Toward half past ten. Ministers have the privilege of not having to stay on after the speeches."

"Were you in formal dress?"

"I took it off before I settled down at this desk."

"You read the report?"

"Yes."

"Did it seem authentic to you?"

The Minister nodded in affirmation.

"It would definitely create a sensation if it were published?"

"Without any doubt."

"Why?"

"Because Professor Calame in fact foretold the disaster. Though I'm in charge of Public Works, I'm incapable of giving you chapter and verse of all his arguments and particularly of the technical details he provides to support his verdict. At any rate, he quite clearly pronounced himself against the entire project, and it was the duty of every person who read the report to vote against the construction of Clairfond as it was planned, or at least to demand a further inquiry. Do you understand?"

"I begin to."

"How the *Rumor* became acquainted with this document I don't know. Have they got another copy? Again I don't know. As far as one can judge the only person in possession of a copy of the Calame report last night was myself."

"What happened then?"

"Toward midnight I telephoned the President of the Council, but I was told that he was at a political meeting in Rouen. I almost called him there."

"You didn't do it?"

"No. Precisely because I was thinking of the lines being tapped. I felt that I was in possession of a case of dynamite capable not only of overthrowing the government, but of dishonoring a number of my colleagues. It is unbelievable that those who had read the report should have been capable of allowing . . ."

Maigret thought he could guess the rest.

"You left the report here in this apartment?"

"Yes."

"In your desk?"

"Yes, it has a lock. I considered that it was safer here than in the Ministry, where there are people coming and going all the time."

"Your driver remained at the door all the time while you studied the file?"

"I sent him away and took a taxi at the corner of the boulevard."

"Did you talk to your wife when you got home?"

"Not about the report. I didn't mention it to anybody until the next day, at one o'clock in the afternoon, when I met the President in the Chamber of Deputies. I put him in the picture; we were standing by the window."

"Was he upset?"

"I think so. Any head of government would have been upset in his place. He asked me to get the report and take it to his study myself."

"The report was no longer in your desk?"

"No."

"And the lock had been tampered with?"

"I don't think so."

"Did you see the President again?"

"No. I felt quite ill. I drove to Boulevard Saint-Germain and canceled all my appointments. My wife telephoned the President and said that I was unwell, that I had collapsed and would go and see him tomorrow morning."

"Does your wife know?"

"For the first time in my life I lied to her. I can't remember what I said to her exactly, and several times I must have floundered."

"Does she know you are here?"

"She believes I am at a meeting. I wonder if you quite understand my situation. I find myself suddenly alone, with the feeling that as soon as I open my mouth, I'll be attacked. Nobody would believe my story. I held the Calame report in my hands. I am the only one, besides Piquemal, to have had it. And at least three times during the last years I have been invited by Arthur Nicoud, the builder in question, to his place in Samois."

Suddenly he slumped. His shoulders seemed narrower, his chin softer. He seemed to be saying:

"Do whatever you like. I have nothing more to say."

Maigret, without asking permission, poured himself some brandy and only after carrying it to his lips remembered to fill the Minister's glass.

2

Probably, at some stage in his own career, Maigret had had a similar experience, but never, he thought, of such intensity. The smallness of the room, its warmth and intimacy, heightened the atmosphere of drama which the smell of the country alcohol, the desk like his father's, the enlarged photographs of the old people on the walls made Maigret feel like a doctor who has been summoned with great urgency and into whose hands the patient has placed his life.

The most surprising thing of all was that the man who was sitting opposite him, as if waiting for the diagnosis, resembled him, if not exactly like a brother, certainly like a cousin. And not only physically. A glance at the family portraits told the Superintendent that his and Auguste Point's origins were very close. Both were born in the country of enlightened peasant stock. Probably the Minister's parents had had the ambition from the time he was born for him to become a doctor or a lawyer, just as Maigret's had done.

Auguste Point had gone beyond their wildest dreams. Were they still alive to know it?

He didn't dare to ask these questions yet. The man in front of him had gone to pieces, and he knew it wasn't because of weakness of character. Looking at him, Maigret was overcome by a complex mixture of emotions: he was angry and disgusted and profoundly discouraged. There had been a time in his own life when he had found himself in a similar situation—although a less dramatic one—and that, too, had had a political background. He had not been guilty. He had acted as it was his duty to act, had behaved not only as an honest man but strictly according to his obligations as a public servant. Nevertheless, in the eyes of almost everyone he had done wrong. He had had to go before a disciplinary council and, as everything was against him, had been blamed. It was at this time that he had to leave the Paris headquarters and found himself exiled to Luçon, in the Vendée, the very department that Auguste Point represented in the Chamber of Deputies. His wife and his friends had told him over and over again that his own conscience was what mattered, but often he seemed to behave, without realizing it, like a guilty man. During those last days at the Quai des Orfèvres, for instance, while his case was being discussed in high places, he did not dare to give any orders to his subordinates, not even to Lucas or to Janvier, and when he came down the main staircase he had kept close to the wall.

Auguste Point was equally incapable of thinking with

any lucidity about his own case. He had just said all that he had to say. During the last hours he had acted as a man who is drowning and believes that only a miracle can save him. Wasn't it strange that it was to Maigret he had appealed, to a man whom he did not know, whom he had never met?

Without realizing it, Maigret had taken on the case, and his questions were those of a doctor trying to make a diagnosis.

"Have you inquired into the identity of Piquemal?"

"I asked my secretary to telephone the School of Civil Engineering, and she was told that Jules Piquemal had been working there for fifteen years as a supervisor."

"Isn't it peculiar that he didn't hand the document to the School Director but brought it to you himself?"

"I don't know. I didn't think about it."

"It seems to indicate that he realized its importance, doesn't it?"

"I think so. Yes."

"In fact, since the Calame report has been rediscovered, Piquemal is the only person, besides yourself, who has had the opportunity of reading it?"

"Not counting the people or person in whose hands it is at the moment."

"We can leave that for the time being. If I'm not mistaken, only one person, besides Piquemal, had known since Tuesday at one o'clock that you were in possession of the document."

"You mean the President of the Council?"

Auguste Point looked at Maigret in dismay. Oscar Malterre was a man of sixty-five who, since he was forty, had in one capacity or another been a member of successive Cabinets. His father had been a mayor, one of his brothers was a deputy and the other a colonial governor.

"I hope you are not suggesting . . ."

"I suggest nothing, Your Excellency. I'm trying to understand. The Calame report was in this desk last night. This afternoon it was no longer there. Are you certain that the door hadn't been forced?"

"You can see for yourself. There is no mark on the wood or on the metal of the keyhole. Could they have used a master key?"

"And the lock of your desk?"

"Have a look. It is not a complicated one. I have often forgotten my key and opened it with a piece of wire."

"Excuse me if I ask you all the usual routine questions, just to clear the air. Who besides yourself has the key to the apartment?"

"My wife, of course."

"You told me that she knows nothing of the Calame affair."

"I didn't talk to her about it. She doesn't even know that I've been here yesterday or today."

"Does she take an active interest in politics?"

"She reads the papers, keeps enough in touch so that we can talk together about my work. When I was first asked to run for deputy, she tried to dissuade me. She didn't want me to become a Cabinet Minister, either. She is not an ambitious woman."

"Does she come from La Roche-sur-Yon?"

"Her father is a lawyer there."

"Let's get back to the keys. Who else has a set?"

"My secretary, Mademoiselle Blanche."

"Blanche who?"

Maigret was making notes in his black notebook.

"Blanche Lamotte. She must be . . . wait a moment . . . forty-one . . . no, forty-two years old."

"Have you known her for a long time?"

"She started to work for me as a typist when she was barely seventeen, just out of school. She has been with me ever since."

"Also from La Roche?"

"From a neighboring village. Her father was a butcher."

"Pretty?"

Auguste Point seemed to ponder over this as though he had never asked himself the question.

"No. I don't think you could say that."

"In love with you?"

Maigret smiled to see the Minister blush.

"How did you know that? Let us say that she's in love in her own way. I don't think there's been a man in her life."

"Jealous of your wife?"

"Not in the usual sense of the word. You might say she's possessive of what she considers to be her territory."

"That means that in the office it is she who is the boss."

Auguste Point was surprised at Maigret's discovering such a simple truth.

"She was in your office, you told me, when Piquemal was announced, and you asked her to leave the room. When you called her back, did you still have the report in your hand?"

"I think so. . . . But I can assure you . . ."

"Your Excellency, please try to understand, I'm blaming nobody, suspecting nobody. Like yourself, I'm trying to find my way. Has anyone else got keys to the apartment?"

"My daughter."

"What age is she?"

"Anne-Marie? Twenty-four."

"Married?"

"Well, she was going to be married next month. With all this about to descend on us, I simply don't know. Do you know the Courmont family?"

"Only by name."

If the Malterres were famous in politics, the Courmonts were equally so in diplomacy and had been, for at least three generations. Robert Courmont, who had a house on Rue de la Faisanderie and was one of the last Frenchmen to wear a monocle, had been an ambassador for more than thirty years, in Tokyo and in London, and was a member of the Institute.

"His son?"

"Yes, Alain Courmont. He's thirty-two years old and has already been attached to three or four embassies, and now he's head of an important department in the Foreign Office. He has been appointed to Buenos Aires; he was to go there three weeks after his marriage. So you can see that the situation is even more complicated than it seems at first glance. A scandal of these dimensions . . . breaking at any moment . . ."

"Does your daughter come here often?"

"Not since we took up residence in the Ministry."

"You mean she's never been here since then?"

"I would prefer to tell you everything, Superintendent. If I don't, it would be pointless to have turned to you. Anne-Marie has graduated in philosophy and literature. She's not a bluestocking, but neither is she like the usual run of young girls today. One day, about a month ago, I found some cigarette ash here. Mademoiselle Blanche doesn't smoke, and neither does my wife. I asked Anne-Marie and she admitted that occasionally she came to the apartment with Alain. I didn't try to find out any more. I remember what she said to me, without blushing, looking me straight in the eye: 'One must be realistic, Father. I'm twenty-four and Alain's thirty-two.' Have you any children, Maigret?"

The Superintendent shook his head.

"I suppose there was no cigarette ash anywhere today?"

"No."

Now that he had only to answer questions, Auguste Point was beginning to look less depressed, like a patient answering a doctor, who knows that the doctor will provide him with some relief in the end. Could Maigret be lingering on this question of the keys on purpose?

"Nobody else?"

"My parliamentary private secretary."

"Who is he?"

"Jacques Fleury."

"You've known him for a long time?"

"I was at the Lycée with him, and later at the University."

"Also from the Vendée?"

"No, he comes from Niert. It isn't far away. He's about my age."

"Lawyer?"

"He never passed his exams."

"Why?"

"He's an odd character. His parents were rich. When he was young, he never wanted regular work. He had a passion for something new every six months. For example, once he took it into his head to run a fishery and he had a few boats. He was also involved in some colonial enterprise that failed. I lost sight of him. When I was elected deputy, I used to see him now and then in Paris."

"Ruined?"

"Completely. He always kept up appearances, he never ceased to do so, nor to be extremely amiable. He is the typical amiable misfit."

"Did he ever ask you any favors?"

"I suppose so, but nothing important. A short time before I became Cabinet Minister, it just happened that I bumped into him more often, and when I found I needed a private secretary he was there, at my disposal."

Auguste Point frowned.

"Since we are on the subject, there is something I'd better explain. You probably cannot imagine what it is like to become a Cabinet Minister all of a sudden. Take my case. I'm a lawyer, a small-town lawyer, of course, but this doesn't minimize my knowledge of the law. Then I was appointed Minister of Public Works. I became, overnight and without any apprenticeship, the head of a Ministry that was full of competent executives, even such illustrious men as Calame. I did what the others do. I assumed an air of confidence. I behaved as if I knew it all. This didn't stop me from feeling a certain irony and hostility around me, and I was also conscious of a number of intrigues of which I understood nothing. Even within the Ministry I'm an outsider, for even there I'm among people who are aware, and have been aware for a long time, of what goes on behind the scenes. To have beside me a man like Fleury, with whom I can relax . . ."

"I understand. When you chose him as your assistant, was he already in touch with the political world?"

"Only through casual encounters in bars and restaurants."

"Married?"

"He has been married. He must still be, because I don't think he ever divorced and he has two children by his wife. They don't live together any longer. He has at least one other entanglement in Paris, maybe two, for he has the gift of complicating his existence."

"You're sure he didn't know you were in possession of the Calame report?"

"He didn't even see Piquemal in the Ministry. I didn't mention anything to him."

"What is the relationship between Fleury and Mademoiselle Blanche?"

"Outwardly cordial. But actually Mademoiselle Blanche cannot stand him, because she is a bourgeoise through and through and Fleury's sentimental life exasperates and upsets her. . . . You see—we are getting nowhere."

"You are quite certain that your wife doesn't suspect that you are here?"

"She noticed, tonight, that I was at the end of my tether. She wanted to get me to bed, since for once I had no important engagement in the evening. I spoke to her about a meeting. . . ."

"Did she believe you?"

"I don't know."

"Are you in the habit of lying to her?"

"No."

It was almost midnight. This time it was the Minister who filled the little stemless glasses and moved, sighing, to the rack to choose a curved pipe with a silver band.

As if confirming Maigret's intuition, the telephone rang. Auguste Point glanced at the Superintendent, wondering if he should answer.

"It's probably your wife. When you get home, you'll be forced to tell her the whole story."

The Minister lifted the receiver.

"Hello. Yes, it's I."

He looked guilty.

"No. I've got someone with me. . . . We had to discuss a very important matter. . . . I'll tell you all about it when I see you. I don't know. . . . It won't be very long. . . . Very well. . . . I assure you I'm perfectly well. . . . What? . . . From the President? . . . He wants me to what? . . . Very well. . . . Yes, I'll do it right away. . . ."

With beads of sweat on his forehead, he turned again to Maigret, the picture of powerless despair.

"There have been three calls from the President's house. . . . The President has asked me to call him at any time. . . ."

He wiped his brow. He even forgot to light his pipe.

"What do I do now?"

"I suggest you telephone him. In any case you'll have

to admit to him tomorrow morning that you no longer have the report. There's not a chance that we can retrieve it overnight."

Point's next remark, which showed his disarray and the instinctive confidence some people have in the power of the police, was almost comical. For he said, almost mechanically:

"You don't think so?"

Then sinking heavily into his chair, he dialed a number that he knew by heart.

"Hello. This is the Minister of Public Works. I'd like to speak to the President. . . . Forgive me, Madame. . . . It's Auguste Point speaking. . . . I believe your husband is expecting . . . Yes. . . . I'll wait. . . ."

He emptied his glass, his eyes fixed on Maigret's waistcoat buttons.

"Yes, Mr. President. . . . Please forgive me for not calling you earlier. . . . I'm better. . . . Yes. . . . It was nothing. . . . Perhaps I was a little tired, yes. . . . Also . . . I was going to tell you . . ."

Maigret could hear a voice at the other end of the line that was in no way reassuring. Auguste Point looked like a child who is being scolded and is trying vainly to justify himself.

"Yes, I know. . . . Believe me. . . ."

At last he was permitted to speak and was searching for the right words.

"You see, something, well, something quite extraordinary has happened. . . . I beg your pardon? . . . It's about the report, yes. . . . I took it yesterday to my private apartment. . . . Yes, Boulevard Pasteur. . . ."

If only he could have been allowed to tell the story

as he wanted to tell it. But he was continually interrupted. He was becoming confused.

"Well, yes. . . . I often come here to work when . . . I can't hear you. Yes, I'm here at the moment. . . . No, no, my wife did not know I was here, or she would have passed on your message at once. . . . No! I've no longer got the Calame report. . . . This is what I've been trying to tell you all the time. I left it here, believing it would be much safer than in the Ministry, and when I came to get it this afternoon, after our conversation . . ."

Maigret turned his head away when he saw tears of humiliation or perhaps irritation drop from the heavy eyelids. "I spent some time searching for it. No, certainly not, I didn't do that!"

With his hand on the receiver, he whispered to Maigret:

"He is asking whether I alerted the police. . . ."

He was listening again—resigned, occasionally mumbling a word or two.

"Yes, yes. . . . I understand. . . ."

His face was bathed in sweat, and Maigret was tempted to go and open the window.

"You have my word, Mr. President. . . ."

The overhead lamp was not lit. The two men and the corner of the study were illuminated only by a lamp with a green shade which left the rest of the room in darkness. From time to time a taxi was heard blowing its horn in the fog on Boulevard Pasteur, and more rarely a train whistled in the distance.

The father's photograph on the wall was that of a

man in his middle sixties, taken probably about ten years earlier, judging by Auguste Point's age. The mother's photograph, on the other hand, was of a woman of barely thirty, with a dress and hair style dating back to the beginning of the century, and Maigret gathered from this that Madame Point, like his own mother, had died when her son was quite small.

There were possibilities that he had not yet mentioned to the Minister and which he was beginning to turn over in his mind. Because of the telephone call, of which he had been the accidental witness, he was thinking of Malterre, the President of the Council, who was also Minister of the Interior and, it followed, had the Criminal Investigation Department in the palm of his hand.

What if Malterre had got wind of Piquemal's visit to Boulevard Saint-Germain and had had Auguste Point followed? Or even after his conversation with Point . . . Anything was possible—that he wanted to get hold of the document to destroy it as well as that he wanted to keep it as his trump card.

The journalistic slang in this case was to the point, the Calame report was a bomb which brought its possessor unbelievable power.

"Yes, Mr. President. . . . Not the police, I repeat. . . ."

The other man was probably badgering him with questions that pushed him further and further out of his depth. His eyes called for Maigret's help, but there was no help forthcoming. He was already slipping. . . .

"The person who is in my study is not here in the capacity of . . ."

After all, he was a strong man, both physically and morally. Maigret, too, knew his own strength and he, too, in the past, had slipped when he had been caught in a much less powerful trap. What had crushed him—he remembered it and would remember it all his life—was the impression of being up against an anonymous force, without name or face, impossible to get hold of. And this force had been no ordinary force, it had been the law.

Auguste Point gave up all reserve.

"It's Superintendent Maigret. . . . I asked him to come and see me privately, I'm certain that he . . ."

He was interrupted. The receiver seemed to vibrate.

"No trail, no. Nobody. . . . No, my wife knows nothing, either. . . . Nor my secretary. I swear to you, Your Excellency."

He forgot about the traditional "Mr. President" and became humble.

"Yes. . . . At nine o'clock, I promise. You want to speak to him? . . . One moment. . . ." Humiliated, he glanced at Maigret.

"The President wishes to . . ."

The Superintendent seized the instrument.

"I'm here, Your Excellency."

"I hear that my colleague of Public Works has told you of the incident?"

"Yes, Your Excellency."

"I needn't underline that the matter must remain absolutely secret. There is no question of starting a regular investigation. Or of informing the Criminal Investigation Department."

"I understand, Your Excellency."

"It is obvious that if you, personally, without any official involvement, without appearing to be interested, should discover anything concerning the Calame report, you'll let me . . ."

He hesitated. He didn't want to be personally implicated. . . .

"You'll let my colleague Point know about it?"

"Yes, Your Excellency."

"That's all."

Maigret wanted to hand the receiver over to the Minister but the line had gone dead.

"I'm sorry, Maigret. He forced me to give your name. I'm told he was a famous prosecutor before entering politics, and I can well believe it. . . . I apologize for putting you in such a position. . . ."

"You're seeing him tomorrow morning?"

"At nine o'clock. He doesn't want the other members of the Cabinet to be informed. What preoccupies him most is whether Piquemal has talked, or will talk, as he is the only one, outside the three of us, who knows that the document has been discovered."

"I'll try to find out what kind of man he is."

"Without disclosing your identity?"

"In all fairness I must warn you that I am bound to talk about it to my chief. I needn't go into any details, by which I mean I needn't mention the Calame report. But it is necessary that he should know that I'm working for you. If it only concerned myself I could tackle the business outside my work. But no doubt I shall need some of my colleagues. . . ."

"Would they have to know everything?"

"They'll know nothing about the report, I promise you."

"I was ready to offer him my resignation, but he took the words out of my mouth. He said that he was not even in a position to dissociate me from the Cabinet because that might, if not reveal the truth, at least arouse suspicions in those who had followed the latest political events. From now on I'm the black sheep, and my colleagues . . ."

"Are you quite certain that the report you had in your hands was in fact a copy of the Calame report?"

Auguste Point raised his head in surprise.

"Do you suggest that it might have a been a falsification?"

"I'm suggesting nothing. I am only considering all the hypotheses. If you are presented with the Calame report, genuine or not, and it disappears immediately afterward, you are automatically discredited (and in fact so is the whole government) because you'll be accused of having suppressed it."

"If this is what was intended, everyone will be talking about it tomorrow."

"Not necessarily so quickly. I would like to know where and in what circumstances it was found."

"Do you think you can do that without anyone knowing?"

"I'll try. I presume, Your Excellency, that you have concealed nothing from me? If I go so far as to ask the question, it's because, in the present circumstances, it's essential that . . ."

"I know. There is one detail that I haven't mentioned

before. I spoke to you, at the beginning, of Arthur Nicoud. When I first met him, I don't remember at what dinner, I was a simple deputy and the idea never crossed my mind that I would find myself one day at the head of Public Works. I knew he was a member of the firm of Nicoud and Sauvegrain, the contractors of Avenue de la République. Arthur Nicoud doesn't live like a businessman, but like a man of the world. Contrary to what one might think, you couldn't call him an upstart, nor is he a typical tycoon. He is well educated. He knows how to live. He goes to the best restaurants in Paris, always surrounded by pretty women, mostly actresses or movie stars.

"I believe that everybody of any importance in the world of letters, arts, politics, has been invited at least once to his Sundays in Samois. I have met many of my colleagues from the Chamber, some press lords and scientists, people whose integrity I'd swear to. Nicoud himself, in his country house, appears to be concerned only with offering his guests the finest food in an elegant background. My wife has never liked him. We have been there about half a dozen times, never alone, never on an intimate footing. On some Sundays there have been about thirty of us lunching at little tables, and then we have gone to the library afterward or got together around the swimming pool.

"What I didn't tell you was that once, I think it was two years ago, yes, two years, at Christmastime, my daughter received a tiny gold fountain pen with her initials on it, accompanied by Arthur Nicoud's card. I almost made her send the present back. I don't remember now to whom I spoke about it, to one of my colleagues, I think, and I was rather angry. He told me that Nicoud's gesture had no significance, that it was an obsession of his, at the end of every year, to send little presents to the daughters or wives of his guests. That year it was fountain pens, which he must have ordered by the dozen. Another year it had been compacts, always in gold, because apparently he has a passion for gold. My daughter kept the fountain pen. I believe she still uses it.

"If the story of the Calame report hits the headlines tomorrow and they say that Auguste Point's daughter has received and accepted . . ."

Maigret nodded slowly. He did not minimize the importance of such a detail.

"Nothing else? He never lent you money?"

Auguste Point blushed to the roots of his hair. Maigret could well understand why. It was not because he had something to reproach himself with, but because, from now on, anyone might put the question to him.

"Never! I swear to you . . ."

"I believe you. You haven't any shares in the company?"

The Minister said no, with a bitter smile.

"I'll do everything I can, beginning tomorrow morning," Maigret promised. "You realize that I know less than you do and that I'm completely unfamiliar with the political world. I also doubt that we'll be able to discover the report before the man who has it now makes use of it. You yourself—would you have suppressed it to save your colleagues if it compromised them?"

"Certainly not."

"What if the head of your party had asked you to?"

"Not even if the President of the Council himself had put it up to me."

"I was more or less certain that that is what you would say. I'm sorry to have asked the question. I'll be going now, Your Excellency."

The two men rose, and Auguste Point stretched out his large, hairy hand.

"I apologize for involving you in all this. I was distraught, at my wits' end. . . ."

Now that his fate was in another man's hands, he felt relieved. He spoke in his normal voice, switched on the overhead light, and opened the door.

"You can't come to see me at the Ministry without arousing curiosity—you're too well known. And you can't telephone because, as I told you before, I suspect my line of being tapped. This apartment is known to everybody. How are we going to keep in touch?"

"I will find some way of communicating with you as soon as it's necessary. You can always telephone me in the evening from a public booth as you did today and, if I'm not there, leave a message with my wife."

They both thought of the same thing, at the same moment, and could not help smiling. Standing by the door they looked very much like conspirators.

"Good night, Your Excellency."

"Thank you, Maigret. Good night."

The Superintendent did not bother to take the elevator. He walked down the four flights, rang for the door to be opened, and found himself back in the fog of the street, which had become thicker and colder. To find a taxi he had to walk to Boulevard Montparnasse. He turned to the right, his pipe between his teeth, his hands in his pockets, and after walking about sixty feet two large lights appeared in front of him and he could hear the engine of a car being started. The fog prevented him from judging the distance. For a moment, Maigret had the impression that the car was coming straight at him, but it only passed by, enveloping him for a few seconds in a yellow glow. He did not have time to raise his hand to hide his face. Besides, he felt sure it would have been useless. No doubt somebody was interested in the person who had paid such a long visit that evening to the Minister's apartment, whose windows above were still lighted up.

With a shrug Maigret went on his way and met only a couple walking slowly, arm in arm, mouth to mouth, who just missed bumping into him.

Eventually he found a taxi. There was still a light in his apartment on Boulevard Richard-Lenoir. He pulled out his key, as always, and as always his wife opened the door before he had time to find the lock. She was in her nightgown, and barefooted; her eyes were swollen with sleep, and she returned at once to the hollow she had made in the bed.

"What time is it?" she asked in a muffled voice.

"Ten minutes past one."

He smiled as he thought that in another, more sumptuous but anonymous apartment another couple was going through the same motions. Auguste Point and his wife were not in their own home. It was not their own home, nor their own bed. They were strangers in the large official building they lived in, which must have seemed to them full of traps.

"What did he want you for?"

"To tell the truth, I don't quite know."

She was only half awake and trying to collect her senses while he was undressing.

"You don't know why he wanted to see you?"

"I should say to seek my advice."

He did not want to use the word "consolation," which would have been more precise. It was funny. It seemed to him that if he were to utter the words "Calame report" here, in the familiar, almost tangible intimacy of his own apartment, he would burst into laughter. At Boulevard Pasteur half an hour ago, the words had been charged with meaning. A Cabinet Minister, with his back to the wall, had spoken them with something like awe. The President of the Council had talked of the report as of a matter of State of the utmost importance. Everything hinged on some thirty pages that had been lying for years in an attic without anyone bothering about them until a school supervisor discovered them perhaps by chance.

"What are you thinking about?"

"About a certain Piquemal."

"Who is that?"

"I don't really know."

It was true that he was thinking of Piquemal, or rather repeating the three syllables of his name and finding them comical.

"Sleep well."

"You, too. Oh, and please wake me at seven o'clock."

"Why so early?"

"I have to telephone someone."

Madame Maigret's hand was already on the switch to put out the light, which was on her side of the bed.

3

A hand gently touched his shoulder and a voice whispered in his ear:

"Maigret! It's seven o'clock."

The smell of the coffee in the cup that his wife was handing to him was invigorating. His senses and his brain began to function rather in the same way as an orchestra does when the musicians try out their instruments in the pit. There was no co-ordination as yet. Seven o'clock, therefore a day different from the others, for usually he got up at eight. Without raising his eyelids he discovered that the day was sunny, whereas yesterday had been cloudy. Even before the idea of fog reminded him of Boulevard Pasteur, he felt a bad taste in his mouth, which had not happened to him for a long time on waking up. He wondered if he was going to have a hangover and thought of the little stemless glasses and the country alcohol from the Minister's home.

Gloomy, he opened his eyes and sat up in bed, reassured to find he had no headache. He had not realized, last night, that they had both drunk a considerable amount.

"Tired?" his wife asked him.

"No. I'll be all right."

His eyes swollen, he sipped his coffee, looking around and muttering in a voice still full of sleep:

"It's a fine day."

"Yes. There's some frost."

The sun had the sharpness and freshness of a rustic white wine. Paris life was starting in Boulevard Richard-Lenoir, with certain familiar noises.

"Must you go out so early?"

"No. But I have to telephone Chabot, and after eight I risk not finding him at home. If it's market day at Fontenay-le-Comte, he may have been out since half past seven."

Julien Chabot, who had become magistrate at Fontenay-le-Comte, where he lived with his mother in the large house where he was born, had been one of his friends from his student days at Nantes, and two years ago, coming back from a conference in Bordeaux, he had dropped in to see him. Old Madame Chabot attended the first Mass, at six in the morning, at seven the house was already humming with life, and at eight Julien went out, not to the Law Courts, where he was by no means burdened with work, but to stroll in the streets of the town or along the Vendée River.

"May I have another cup?"

He drew the telephone to his side and dialed the operator. As the operator was repeating the number he suddenly thought that if one of his hypotheses of the night before was correct his telephone must already be tapped. This irritated him. Once again he experienced the revulsion that had seized him when much against his will he himself had become involved in a political intrigue. And with it came a sense of grievance against Auguste Point, whom he did not know from Adam, whom he had never met before, and who had found it necessary to appeal to Maigret to get him out of a mess.

"Madame Chabot? . . . Hello! . . . Is this Madame Chabot speaking? . . . This is Maigret speaking . . . No! Maigret. . . ."

She was somewhat deaf. He had to repeat his name five or six times and explain:

"Jules Maigret, the police . . ."

Then she exclaimed:

"You're in Fontenay?"

"No, I'm calling from Paris. Is your son there?"

She spoke too loud, too close to the instrument. He didn't hear what she was saying. More than a minute passed before he recognized his friend's voice.

"Julien?"

"Yes."

"Can you hear me?"

"As clearly as if you were speaking from the station. How are you?"

"Very well. Listen to me. I'm disturbing you because I need some information. Were you having your breakfast?"

"Yes. But it doesn't matter."

"You know Auguste Point?"

"You mean the Cabinet Minister?"

"Yes."

"I used to see him often when he was a lawyer at La Roche-sur-Yon."

"What do you think of him?"

"He is a remarkable man."

"Give me some details. Anything that comes into your mind."

"His father, Evariste Point, owns a well-known hotel at Sainte-Hermine, Clemenceau's town; famous not for its rooms, but for its cuisine. Real lovers of good food came from all over the place to eat there. He must be almost ninety. Some years ago he made over the business to his son-in-law and to his daughter, but he still keeps an eye on it. Auguste Point, his only son, was graduated at about the same time we were, but at Poitiers. Are you still there?"

"Yes."

"Shall I go on? He was a prodigious worker, a real grind. He opened a law office, in Town Hall Square, at La Roche-sur-Yon. You know the town. He was there for years, mostly involved in litigation work between farmers and landowners. He married the daughter of a solicitor, Arthur Belion, who died two or three years ago and whose widow still lives at La Roche. I think, if there hadn't been a war, Auguste Point would have continued peacefully as an attorney in the Vendée and in Poitiers. During the occupation one heard very little about him; his life went on as if nothing unusual was happening. Everybody was surprised when, a few weeks before they retreated, the Germans arrested him and took him to Niort, and then to somewhere in Alsace. They caught three or four other people at the same time, one of them a surgeon from Bressuires, and it was then that we learned that throughout the war Auguste Point had hidden British agents and pilots escaped from German camps in the farm he owns near La Roche.

"He came back, emaciated and a sick man, a few days after the liberation. He did not try to push himself, or worm his way onto committees, nor did he march in any procession. You remember the chaos there was at the time. Politics got mixed up in it, too. Nobody could tell the saints from the sinners. Finally, in all the confusion, they turned to him. He did some good work and always with no fuss, without getting a swollen head, and in the end we sent him to Paris as deputy. That's more or less the entire story. The Points have kept their house in the town. They live in Paris when the Chamber is in session, then come back as soon as possible, and Auguste has kept many of his clients. I believe that his wife helps him a lot. They have a daughter."

"I know."

"Well then, you know as much as I do."

"Do you know his secretary?"

"Mademoiselle Blanche? I often saw her in his office. We call her the Dragon because of the ferocity with which she protects her employer."

"Nothing more about her?"

"I presume she's in love with him, in the way of aging spinsters."

"She worked for him before she was an aging spinster."

"I know. But that's another matter, and I can't help you there. What's the trouble?"

"Nothing yet. Do you know a certain Jacques Fleury?"

"Slightly. I met him two or three times, but it must have been twenty years ago, at least. He must be living in Paris. I don't know what he is doing."

"Thank you, and again forgive me for taking you away from your breakfast."

"My mother's keeping it warm."

Not knowing what more to say, Maigret added:

"Is the weather good, down there?"

"There's some sun, but there's frost on the roofs."

"It's cold here, too. See you soon, old boy. Give my regards to your mother."

For Julien Chabot, this telephone call was an event, and he was going to ponder over it on his stroll in the streets of the town, wondering why Maigret was so interested in the comings and goings of the Minister of Public Works.

The Superintendent's breakfast was accompanied by a lingering aftertaste of alcohol, and when he went out he decided to walk, and stopped at a bar on Place de la République in order to settle his stomach with a generous glass of white wine.

He bought all the morning papers, something he did not usually do, and arrived at the Quai des Orfèvres just in time for the daily report. While his colleagues were gathered in the boss's office he said nothing, did not really listen, but idly contemplated the Seine and the passers-by on the Pont Saint-Michel. He alone remained behind when the others left. The boss knew what that meant.

"What is it, Maigret?"

"Trouble."

"In the Department?"

"No. Paris has never been so calm as it's been these last five days. But last night I was summoned in person by a Cabinet Minister, and he's asked me to take on a matter I don't like. There was nothing I could do but accept. I warned him I would talk to you about it, but without giving you any details."

The Chief of Police frowned.

"It smells?"

"Yes, very much so."

"Connected with the Clairfond disaster?"

"Yes."

"And a Cabinet Minister has personally entrusted you . . ."

"The President of the Council has been informed."

"I don't want to know any more. Get on with it, old boy, if you have to. But watch your step."

"I'll try to."

"Do you need any men?"

"Yes, definitely, three or four. They won't know precisely what it's about."

"Why didn't he get in touch with Criminal Investigation?"

"You don't understand?"

"I do. That's why I'm not happy about you. Well . . ."

Maigret went to his office and opened the door leading into the inspectors' room.

"Will you come in for a moment, Janvier?" Then seeing Lapointe about to leave the room:

"Are you on anything important?"

"No, sir. Just routine jobs."

"Pass them on to someone else and wait for me. You too, Lucas."

Back in his office with Janvier, he closed the door.

"I'm going to give you a hell of a difficult assignment, old fellow. There won't be any report to write, or any account to give to anyone but myself. If you make a mistake, it may cost you quite a bit."

Janvier smiled, pleased to be entrusted with a delicate matter.

"The Minister of Public Works has a secretary called Blanche Lamotte, about forty-three years old."

He had pulled his black notebook out of his pocket.

"I don't know where she lives or what her working hours are. I want to know all about her—the kind of life she leads outside the Ministry and the people she meets. Neither she, nor anyone else, must suspect that the Police Department is interested in her. Perhaps if you watch the staff leaving the building, at noon, you'll be able to discover where she lunches. See what you can do. If she notices you're taking an interest, you'll have to play up to her, if necessary."

Janvier, who was married and had just had his fourth child, made a face.

"Very well, sir. I'll do my best. There's nothing specific that you want me to find out?"

"I want everything you can find out, and then I'll see what I can make of it."

"Is it urgent?"

"Very urgent. You won't mention it to anyone, not even to Lapointe or Lucas. Is that clear?"

He went to the communicating door and opened it again.

"Lapointe! Come here."

Lapointe, the little fellow, as everyone called him because he was the last to join the staff and looked more like a student than a policeman, had already gathered that this was to be a confidential mission and was clearly excited about it.

"You know the School of Civil Engineering?"

"Yes, Rue des Saints-Pères. I used to lunch in a small restaurant almost opposite it for a long time."

"Very well. There's a supervisor there, called Piquemal. His first name is Jules, like mine. I don't know whether he lives in the school or not. I know nothing about him, and I want to know as much as possible."

He repeated more or less what he had said to Janvier.

"For some reason, from the description I've had of him, he gives me the impression of being unmarried. Perhaps he lives in a small hotel. In that case, take a room in the hotel and pretend you're a student."

Then it was Lucas's turn, and there were similar instructions, except that Lucas was assigned to Jacques Fleury, the Minister's parliamentary secretary.

The three inspectors rarely had their photographs in the paper. The general public did not know them, or more precisely, of the three it knew Lucas but only by name.

Of course if Criminal Investigation had had a hand in the business, they would be recognized immediately, but that was inevitable. Besides, in that case, as Maigret had already decided that morning, his telephone conversations, whether from his home or from the Quai des Orfèvres, were being monitored by the Rue des Saussaies.

Somebody, the night before, had deliberately shone his lights on him, and if this someone knew Auguste Point's refuge, knew that he was there that night and had a visitor, he was also bound to be able to recognize Maigret at first sight.

Alone in his office, he opened the window as if being involved in this matter had given him a longing for a breath of fresh air. The papers were on the table. He was on the point of looking at them, then decided to deal first with current affairs, sign warrants and the usual reports.

This made him feel almost a tenderness for the small thieves, the maniacs, the swindlers, the delinquents of every variety with whom he usually had to deal.

After making several phone calls, he went back to the inspectors' room to give instructions which had no connection with Point or the wretched Calame report.

By now, Auguste Point must have already seen the President. Had he told his wife the whole story before he went, as the Superintendent had advised him to do?

It was cooler than he had expected, and he had to shut the window. He installed himself in his chair and opened the first newspaper in the pile. They were all still full of the Clairfond disaster and all, whatever party they belonged to, were forced, because of public opinion, to press for an inquiry.

The majority blamed Arthur Nicoud. One of the articles carried the headline: "The Nicoud-Sauvegrain Monopoly." It published a list of the works entrusted to the firm on Avenue de la République over recent years by the government and by certain municipalities. The cost of the works was given in columns on the opposite page and the total reached several billions.

Then in conclusion:

It would be interesting to establish the list of officials, Ministers, deputies, senators, town councilors of the city of Paris and others who have been Arthur Nicoud's guests in his luxurious property in Samois.

Perhaps a careful study of the tabs of Mr. Nicoud's check-books would be revealing.

One paper, the *Globe,* which was, if not owned, certainly inspired by the deputy Mascoulin, had a headline in the style of Zola's famous "J'accuse":

IS IT TRUE THAT . . . ?

And a number of questions followed, in larger print than usual in a layout that made the text conspicuous.

Is it true that the idea of the Clairfond Sanatorium was not born in the minds of legislators anxiously concerned with children's health, but in the mind of a dealer in concrete?

Is it true that this idea had been introduced five years previously to a number of high-placed officials over luxurious lunches given by that dealer in concrete at his property in Samois?

Is it true that not only did they find there excellent food and wine, but that the guests emerged from their host's private study with fat checks in their pockets?

Is it true that when the project took shape, all those who knew the site chosen for the remarkable sanatorium realized the folly and the danger of the enterprise?

Is it true that the parliamentary commission in charge of investigation, and presided over by the brother of the present President of the Council, decided to request the expert opinion of an authority of untarnished reputation?

Is it true that that expert, Julien Calame, professor of applied mechanics and civil architecture at the National School of Civil Engineering, spent three weeks on the site with the plans . . . that on his return he handed over to those concerned a report that was catastrophic for the supporters of the project . . . that nevertheless the funds were allocated and the construction of Clairfond started a few weeks later?

Is it true that up to his death, two years ago, Julien Calame, according to all who saw him, gave the impression of a man with a weight on his conscience?

Is it true that in his report he foresaw the Clairfond disaster almost exactly as it happened?

Is it true that the Calame report, which must have existed in a number of copies, has disappeared from the archives of the Chamber of Deputies as well as from those of several interested Ministries?

Is it true that since the disaster at least thirty government employees live in terror that a copy of the report may be found?

Is it true that, in spite of all precautions, it has been found at a very recent date?

. . . and that this resurrected copy has been handed over to those concerned?

Then, in a further headline across the page:

WE WANT TO KNOW

Is the Calame report still in the hands of the person to whom it was given? Or has it been destroyed to save the gang of compromised politicians? If that is not the case—

where is it at the moment of writing and why has it not yet been published, when public opinion justifiably demands the punishment of those guilty of a disaster that has cost the lives of one hundred and twenty-eight young Frenchmen?

And at the end of the page, in the same print as the two preceding headlines:

WHERE IS THE CALAME REPORT?

Maigret found himself wiping his sweating forehead. It was not difficult to imagine Auguste Point's reaction on reading the article.

The *Globe* did not have a large circulation. It was an independent paper. Nor did it represent any of the big parties, only a small fraction, of which Joseph Mascoulin was the leader.

But the other papers would certainly set in motion their own independent inquiries, to discover the truth. And this truth Maigret, too, wished to discover, provided it was discovered in its entirety.

He had, however, the impression that it was not what the *Globe* was searching for. If Mascoulin, for instance, was the man in whose hands the report was at the moment, why did he not publish it in letters as large as his article? He would have immediately provoked a ministerial crisis, a radical sweep of the parliamentarian ranks, and he would have appeared to the public as the defender of the people's interests and of political ethics.

For a man who had always worked in the background this was a unique opportunity to achieve great prominence and probably play a tremendous part in the years to come. If he was in possession of the document, why did he not publish it?

It was Maigret's turn to put the questions.

If Mascoulin did not have it, how did he know that the report had been found?

How had he learned that Piquemal had handed it over to an official personage?

And why did he suspect that Auguste Point had not transmitted it higher up?

Maigret had no desire to penetrate or to have knowledge of the shady side of politics. But he did not have to know much about the intrigues that simmer behind the scenes to be aware of the following:

1. That it was in a dubious if not blackmailing newssheet, the *Rumor*, owned by Hector Tabard, that the Calame report had been mentioned three times after the Clairfond disaster.

2. That the discovery of the report had followed this publication in rather strange circumstances.

3. That Piquemal, a simple supervisor at the National School of Engineering, had gone directly to the Minister instead of going through the proper channels, in this case, approaching the director of the school.

4. That Joseph Mascoulin had become aware of this operation.

5. That he seemed equally aware of the disappearance of the report.

Were Mascoulin and Tabard playing the same game? Were they playing it together or each on his own account?

Maigret went to open the window again and stood

for a long time looking at the Seine, smoking his pipe. Never had he had to deal with such a complicated case, with so little evidence at his disposal.

When the crime was a burglary or a murder he was at once on familiar ground. Here, on the contrary, it was a question of people whose names and reputations he knew only vaguely from the newspapers. He knew, for instance, that Mascoulin lunched every day at the same table in a restaurant on Place des Victoires called "Filet de Sole" where a constant stream of people came to shake his hand and whisper some information to him. Mascoulin was believed to know all there was to know about the private life of all the politicians. He was rarely challenged, and his name appeared in the papers only on the eve of an important issue. Then one might read:

"The deputy Mascoulin predicts that the proposal will be adopted by three hundred and forty-two votes."

Professionals took these prognostications most seriously, for Mascoulin was rarely mistaken, and then never by more than two or three votes.

He was not on any commissions, did not preside over any committee, nevertheless he was more feared than the leader of a big party.

Maigret decided that he would go at noon to the Filet de Sole and lunch there, if only to see at closer quarters the man of whom he had had but a glimpse on official occasions.

Mascoulin was a bachelor, though he was over forty. His name was not associated with any girl friend. He was never seen at receptions, theaters, or night clubs. He had a long, bony head, and at noon he already seemed to need a shave. He dressed indifferently; his clothes were never pressed and always seemed to be in need of cleaning.

Why, from Auguste Point's description of Piquemal, did Maigret think that this man was of rather the same type?

He was wary of solitary men, people without an acknowledged passion.

Finally he decided against lunching at the Filet de Sole; it would have seemed too much like a declaration of war. Instead, he made his way to the Brasserie Dauphine, where he found two colleagues with whom he managed for an hour to talk of things other than the Calame report.

One of the afternoon papers had taken up the theme of the *Globe* in a much more prudent manner, with veiled insinuations, clamoring only for the truth about the Calame report. One of the editors had tried to interview the President of the Council himself on the subject but was unable to get through to him. Auguste Point was not mentioned, for the building of the sanatorium was in fact the business of the Ministry of Public Health.

At three o'clock there was a knock on Maigret's door. He growled and immediately it was opened, and Lapointe came in, looking rather worried.

"You've got news?"

"Nothing definite, sir. Up to now it's all been a matter of chance."

"Give me all the details."

"I tried to follow your instructions. You'll tell me if I made mistakes. First I telephoned the National School of Civil Engineering, pretending that I was a cousin of

Piquemal's and that I had just arrived in Paris and wanted to see him but didn't have his address."

"Did they give it to you?"

"Without the slightest hesitation. He lives at the Hôtel du Berry, Rue Jacob. It's a modest hotel with about thirty rooms, and the owner herself does most of the cleaning, while her husband does the accounts. I went back home to get a suitcase and presented myself at Rue Jacob as a student, as you suggested. I was lucky, there was a free room, and I took it for a week. It was about half past ten when I came down and stopped at the office to have a chat with the proprietor."

"Did you mention Piquemal?"

"Yes, I told him that I had seen him during the holidays and remembered that he lived here."

"What did he tell you?"

"That he was out. He leaves the hotel every morning at eight o'clock and goes to a small bar to have his coffee and croissants. He has to be in the school at half past eight."

"Does he return to the hotel during the day?"

"No. He comes back regularly at about half past seven, goes to his room, and goes out again only a couple of times a week. It seems he is leading the most regular kind of life, never entertains anyone, sees no women, doesn't smoke or drink, and spends his evenings and sometimes part of the night reading."

Maigret sensed that Lapointe had more to say and waited patiently.

"Perhaps I made a mistake, but I thought I was doing the right thing. When I discovered that his room was on the same floor as mine and got the number, I thought you would like to know what was inside it. During the day the hotel is almost always empty. There was only someone playing the saxophone on the third floor, probably a musician practicing, and I could hear the servant on the floor above me. I tried my key. They are simple keys, an old-fashioned type. It didn't work at first, but I fiddled about a bit and managed to open the door."

"I hope Piquemal didn't happen to be at home."

"No. If they search for my fingerprints they'll find them everywhere, because I didn't wear gloves. I opened the drawers, the cupboard, and an unlocked suitcase as well, hidden in a corner. Piquemal has only one extra suit, dark gray, and a pair of black shoes. His comb has got half its teeth missing and his toothbrush is ancient. He doesn't use cream to shave himself, only a brush. The proprietor is right when he says that he spends his evenings reading. There are books all over the place, particularly books on philosophy, political economy, and history. Most of them have been bought secondhand on the *quais*. Three or four of them come from public libraries. I copied a few of the authors' names. Engels, Spinoza, Kierkegaard, St. Augustine, Karl Marx, Father Sertillange, Saint-Simon. . . . Does it make any sense to you?"

"It does. Go on."

"There was a cardboard box in one of the drawers containing membership cards, old and new, some from twenty years back, some of quite recent date. The oldest was for the Association of the Croix de Feu. Another one, dated 1937, was for the Action Française.* Immediately after the war Piquemal joined a branch of the

* Ultra-right-wing groups.

Communist Party. The card was renewed for three years."

Lapointe was consulting his notes.

"He also belonged to the International Theosophical League, based in Switzerland. You've heard of it?"

"Yes."

"I forgot to tell you two of the books were about yoga and there was a manual of judo as well."

Judging by all this, Piquemal had experimented with all manner of philosophical and social theories. All extremist parties have members like him who march behind the banners staring fixedly ahead.

"That's all?"

"So far as his room is concerned, yes. No letters. When I came down, I asked the proprietor whether he ever got any mail and he replied that he'd never seen anything except prospectuses and circulars. I went to the bistro at the corner. Unfortunately, it was the apéritif hour. The bar was crowded. I had to wait for a long time and have two drinks before I could speak to the owner without becoming conspicuous. I told him the same story: that I came from the provinces and was anxious to see Piquemal.

" 'The professor?' he asked, which seemed to indicate that in certain circles Piquemal assumed the rank of a professor.

" 'If you had come at eight o'clock . . . By now he must be busy teaching. . . . I don't know where he has lunch.'

" 'Did he come this morning?'

" 'I saw him at the croissant basket, as usual. He always eats three. But today somebody I don't know, and who had arrived before him, went up to him and started to talk with him. Generally, Piquemal is not forthcoming. He must have too many things on his mind to waste his time with gossip. He's polite, but cold—you know the kind of "Good morning. How much is that? Good-by." It doesn't bother me because I have other clients like him, people who work with their minds, and I can imagine what it's like. But what surprised me was to see Monsieur Piquemal leave with the stranger and, instead of turning to the left as he usually does, they turned right.' "

"What was the other man like? Did he describe him?"

"Not very well. A man of about forty, looking like a minor official or a traveling salesman. He walked in without saying anything, a little before eight, went to the counter, and ordered a cup of coffee. No beard or mustache. On the heavy side."

Maigret could not help thinking that this could be the description of some dozen of inspectors from the Rue des Saussaies.

"Is that all you know?"

"Yes. After lunch I called up the School of Civil Engineering again and asked for Piquemal. This time I didn't tell them who I was and they didn't ask me. But they replied that he hadn't been seen the entire day."

"Is he on holiday?"

"No. He simply didn't turn up. What is most astonishing is that he didn't telephone to say he would be absent. It's the first time it's ever happened. I went back to the Hôtel du Berry and to my room. Then I went and knocked at Piquemal's door. I opened it. There was nobody there. Nothing had been moved since my first visit. You've asked me for all the details. I went to the school, playing the role of friend from the provinces. I learned where he lunches—about a hundred yards away, Rue des Saints-Pères, in a Norman restaurant. I went there. Piquemal hadn't come for lunch today. I saw his napkin with a numbered ring on it and a half-finished bottle of mineral water on his usual table. That's all, sir. Did I do anything wrong?"

What prompted him to ask the last question, in some anxiety, was that Maigret's forehead had a frown on it and his face was troubled. Was this affair going to end the same way as his first entanglement with politics, which had landed him in disgrace in Luçon? That other time, too, the cause of it all had been a certain rivalry between the Rue des Saussaies and the Quai des Orfèvres, each of the police departments receiving different directives, each defending opposing interests whether they liked it or not because of a struggle in high places.

At midnight the President of the Council had learned that Auguste Point had approached Maigret.

At eight in the morning Piquemal, the man who had discovered the Calame report, had been approached by a stranger in the little bar where he peacefully drank his coffee, and he had followed the man without any hesitation, without an argument.

"You've done good work, my boy."

"No mistakes?"

"I don't think so."

"And now?"

"I don't know. Perhaps you'd better stay on in the Hôtel du Berry, in case Piquemal returns."

"In that case, I'll telephone you."

"Yes, here or at home."

One of the men who had read the Calame report had disappeared.

Auguste Point, who had read it too, was still around, but he was a Cabinet Minister and therefore more difficult to spirit away.

At the very thought of it, Maigret seemed to taste again the drink he had had the night before, and all he wanted was a glass of beer somewhere among ordinary people with ordinary little problems.

4

Maigret was on his way back from the Brasserie Dauphine, where he had gone to have a glass of beer, when he saw Janvier proceeding rapidly toward Police Headquarters.

It was almost hot, in the middle of the afternoon. The sun had lost its dimness, and for the first time this year Maigret had left his coat at the office. He called "Hey!" two or three times. Janvier stopped, saw him, and turned back to meet him.

"Would you like a drink?"

For no particular reason, the Superintendent was reluctant to go straight back to the Quai des Orfèvres. The spring, probably, had something to do with it, and also the atmosphere of tension in which he had lived since the day before.

Janvier had a comic look on his face, the look of a

man who is not quite sure whether he is going to get a scolding or be patted on the back. Instead of staying by the bar, they went to the back room, which at this time of day was empty.

"A beer?"

"If you'd like."

They remained silent, waiting to be served.

"We aren't the only ones trailing the little lady, Chief," Janvier murmured. "I noticed that there are quite a few of us interested in her movements."

"Tell me the whole business."

"First thing this morning, I had a look around near the Ministry, on Boulevard Saint-Germain. I got within about twenty feet of it when I saw Rougier standing on the opposite sidewalk, and apparently taking a keen interest in the sparrows."

Both men knew Gaston Rougier, an inspector from the Rue des Saussaies with whom they were, actually, on the best of terms. He was a decent fellow, who lived in the suburbs and always had his pockets full of photographs of his seven or eight children.

"Did he see you?"

"Yes."

"Did he speak to you?"

"The street was almost empty. I couldn't possibly avoid him. When I got up to him, he asked me:

" 'You, too?'

"I acted the fool and asked:

" 'Me, too, what?'

"Then he winked at me.

" 'Nothing. I'm not asking you to let the cat out of the bag. I'm surprised to see so many familiar faces about, this morning, that's all. It's just bad luck that there's not even a bistrot opposite this blasted Ministry.'

"From where we were standing we could see into the courtyard, and I recognized Ramire, of Intelligence, who seemed to be getting on like a house afire with the concierge.

"I kept up the acting and went on my way. I didn't stop till I got to a café on Rue Solférino and tried my luck with the telephone directory. I found Blanche Lamotte's name and her address, 63, Rue Vaneau. It was only a stone's throw away."

"And there again you bumped into Criminal Investigation?"

"Not quite. You know Rue Vaneau, it's quiet, almost provincial, it even has a few trees in the gardens. Number 63 is an unpretentious apartment house, but quite comfortable. The concierge was in her room, peeling potatoes.

" 'Is Mademoiselle Lamotte at home?' I asked.

"I could tell at once she was looking at me somewhat quizzically. However, I ignored this.

" 'I'm an inspector from an insurance company,' I said. 'Mademoiselle Lamotte has applied for life insurance, and I'm just checking.' She didn't actually burst out laughing, but very nearly. And then she asked me:

" 'How many different branches of the police are there in Paris?'

" 'I don't know what you mean.'

" 'As to you, I've seen you before with a fat superintendent, whose name I've forgotten, when the little lady of fifty-seven took an overdose of sleeping pills two years ago. This time all your colleagues have been at it.'

" 'Have many of them been here, then?' I asked.

" 'There was one yesterday morning.'

" 'Did he show you his badge?'

" 'I didn't ask him for it. I'm not asking for yours, either. I'm quite capable of recognizing a policeman when I see one.'

" 'Did he ask you a lot of questions?'

" 'Four or five: whether she lived alone, if she was visited sometimes by a man of about fifty, on the fat side. . . . I said no.'

" 'Is that the truth?'

" 'It is. Also if she often had a brief case when she came home. I told him she did sometimes, that she also has a typewriter upstairs in her apartment and that she often brings work back in the evening. I suppose that you know as well as I do that she's a Cabinet Minister's secretary.'

" 'I'm aware of it, yes.'

" 'He also wanted to know if she had had her brief case with her last night. I had to admit that I hadn't noticed. Then he pretended to be going away. I went up to the first floor where I go every day, to oblige an old lady. I heard him on the stairs a little later on, but I didn't let on I was there. But I do know that he stopped at the third floor, where Mademoiselle Blanche lives, and that he got into her apartment.'

" 'And you let him do that?'

" 'I've been a concierge long enough to have learned not to be on bad terms with the police.'

" 'Did he stay there for a long time?'

" 'About ten minutes.'

" 'Did you see him again?'

" 'Not that one.'

" 'Did you speak to the lady about it?' "

Maigret was listening, staring hard at his glass, trying to fit the incident in with the events that he already knew. Janvier went on:

"She hesitated. She felt herself blushing and decided to tell me the truth.

" 'I told her that someone had been here asking questions about her and had gone up to her floor. I didn't mention the police.'

" 'Did she seem surprised?'

" 'For a moment, yes. Then she murmured: "I think I know what it's about."

" 'As for the ones who came this morning, a few minutes after she had gone to work—there were two of them. They also told me that they were from the police. The smaller one wanted to show me his badge, but I didn't look at it.'

" 'Did they go up too?'

" 'No. They asked me the same questions and some others as well.'

" 'What others?'

" 'Whether she goes out a lot, who with, who her friends are, male and female, whether she does a lot of telephoning, whether . . .' "

Maigret interrupted the inspector:

"What did she tell you about her?"

"She gave me the name of one of her friends, a certain Lucile Cristin who lives in the neighborhood, who most likely works in an office and has a squint. Mademoiselle Blanche lunches in a restaurant called the Three Ministries, on Boulevard Saint-Germain. In the evening she cooks her own dinner. This Lucile Cristin often comes to eat with her. I've not been able to find her address. The concierge also told me about another friend, who doesn't often go to Rue Vaneau, but whom Mademoiselle Blanche goes to dine with every Sunday. She's married to a commissioner in the Halles called Hariel, and lives on Rue de Courcelles. The concierge believes she comes from La Roche-sur-Yon, like Mademoiselle Blanche."

"Did you go to Rue de Courcelles?"

"I gathered from you I was to leave no stone unturned. As I don't even know what it is all about . . ."

"Go on."

"Her information was correct. I went to Madame Hariel's apartment; she lives comfortably, has three children; the youngest is eight. I put on the insurance agent act again. She had no suspicions and I concluded that I was the first to go and see her. She knew Blanche Lamotte in La Roche, where they went to school together. They had lost sight of one another and met accidentally in Paris three years ago. Madame Hariel invited her friend to her home and now she goes there to dine every Sunday. Nothing of any interest besides that. Blanche Lamotte leads a regular life, entirely devoted to her work, and talks enthusiastically about her boss—she would obviously die for him."

"That's all?"

"No. About a year ago, Blanche asked Hariel if he knew of any vacant job for a friend of hers, who was in difficulties. It was Fleury. Hariel, who seems to be a kind-hearted man, gave him some work in his office. Fleury had to be there every day at six in the morning."

"What happened?"

"He came to work for three days, and after that they never saw him again and he didn't even apologize. Mademoiselle Blanche was very embarrassed by the whole thing and apologized profusely for him. I went back to Boulevard Saint-Germain with the idea of looking in at the Three Ministries. But long before I got there, I could see not only Gaston Rougier still on duty but one of his colleagues as well. I've forgotten his name."

Maigret was trying hard to put all this information into some kind of pattern. On Monday evening Auguste Point had gone to his apartment on Boulevard Pasteur and had left the Calame report there, believing it to be in a safer place than elsewhere.

On Tuesday morning someone who pretended to be from the police had appeared at Rue Vaneau, where Mademoiselle Blanche lived, and after having asked the concierge some questions of no importance had managed to get himself into her apartment. Was he really from the police? If he was, the whole business had an even more unpleasant twist to it than the Superintendent had anticipated. However, he had a feeling that this first visit had nothing to do with the Rue des Saussaies. Was it the same man who, finding nothing in the secretary's apartment, had gone on to Boulevard Pasteur and taken the document from there?

"She didn't describe him to you?"

"Only vaguely. An ordinary person—neither young nor old, rather stout, with enough practice in questioning for her to take him for a policeman."

This was almost the same description that the owner of the bar on Rue Jacob had given of the man who had approached Piquemal and had left with him. As for this morning's little bunch—the ones who had not gone to the secretary's apartment—it seemed likely they would be from the Criminal Investigation Department.

"What am I to do now?"

"I don't know."

"Oh, I forgot; as I recrossed Boulevard Saint-Germain I thought I caught a glimpse of Lucas in a bar."

"It could have been he. . . ."

"Is he on the same case?"

"More or less."

"Am I to go on taking an interest in the lady?"

"We'll see after I've talked to Lucas. Wait here for a moment."

Maigret went to the telephone and called Police Headquarters.

"Is Lucas back?"

"Not yet."

"Is that you, Torrence? As soon as he turns up, send him to the Brasserie Dauphine."

A boy was passing in the street with the latest edition of the afternoon papers, which carried large headlines, and as Maigret walked to the door he searched for some change in his pocket. When he came back and sat down beside Janvier he spread out the paper. The headline running across the entire page said:

HAS ARTHUR NICOUD ESCAPED?

The news was sensational enough for the paper to have altered its front page.

The Clairfond case has reopened in an unexpected manner, though there are those who ought to have foreseen it. It is known that the day after the disaster public opinion was greatly upset and demanded a thorough investigation of those responsible for it. The Nicoud and Sauvegrain concern, which five years ago built the now all too famous sanatorium, should have been made, according to those in the know, the object of a minute and immediate inquiry. Why has nothing been done? This is what we hope will be explained in the next few days. However, Arthur Nicoud, afraid of appearing in public, has considered it safer to seek refuge in a hunting lodge he owns in Sologne. The police were apparently aware of it. We have even been assured that it was, in fact, the police who suggested to the contractor that he should disappear for a time from the public eye, in order to avoid any incident. Only this morning, four weeks after the disaster, has it been decided in high places to summon Arthur Nicoud and question him on matters that are of burning interest to everyone. Early this morning two inspectors from the Criminal Investigation Department went to the lodge, where they found no one but the gamekeeper. He told the officers that his master had left the night before for an unknown destination. But it did not remain unknown for long. Two hours ago, in fact, our special correspondent in Brussels telephoned to say that Arthur Nicoud had arrived in the town later this morning and occupies a luxurious suite in the Hôtel Metropole. Our correspondent succeeded in approaching him and put to him the following questions, which we reproduce verbatim together with the replies.

"Is it true that you left your lodge in Sologne so abruptly because you were warned that the police were coming to visit you?"

"It is completely untrue. I knew and know nothing about the intentions of the police; for the last month they have known perfectly well where to find me."

"Did you leave France because you could foresee new developments?"

"I came to Brussels because I have some building projects here that necessitate my presence."

"What building projects?"

"The construction of an airport which I have undertaken."

"Do you intend to go back to France and place yourself at the disposal of the authorities?"

"I have no intention of changing my plans in any way."

"Do you mean that you will remain in Brussels until the Clairfond case is forgotten?"

"I repeat that I'm staying here as long as my business keeps me here."

"Even if a summons were issued for you to return?"

"The police had a whole month in which to question me. It isn't my fault if they haven't done so!"

"You have heard about the Calame report?"

"I don't know what you are talking about."

At this point Arthur Nicoud put an end to the conversation, which our correspondent immediately telephoned to us. It seems—though we were unable to confirm it—that an elegant, fair-haired young woman arrived an hour after Nicoud and was shown immediately to his apartment, where she probably is at the moment. In the Rue des Saussaies, it has been confirmed that two inspectors went to Sologne to question the contractor on several matters. When we mentioned a summons to return, we were told that there could be no question of that at the moment.

"Is that the case we're working on?" Janvier muttered with a sour expression.

"It is."

He opened his mouth, probably to ask how it had happened that Maigret had agreed to be mixed up with such an unsavory political case. But he said nothing. Lucas could be seen crossing the square, slightly dragging his left leg as usual. He did not stop at the bar, but came and sat opposite the two men, wiping the sweat from his face and looking gloomy.

Pointing to the paper, he said in an aggrieved voice, which he had never before used in Maigret's presence:

"I've just read it."

The Superintendent felt a twinge of guilt as he faced his colleagues. Lapointe had probably also discovered by now what it was all about.

"A beer?" offered Maigret.

"No. A Pernod."

And this was not characteristic of Lucas, either. They waited to be served before they began to talk in an undertone.

"I suppose you bumped into the men from the Big House everywhere you went?" It was their way of describing Criminal Investigation.

"You might have warned me to be discreet," grumbled Lucas. "If it is a question of getting ahead of them, I can tell you right away they're way up in front."

"Tell us."

"Tell you what?"

"What you've been up to."

"I started to stroll up and down Boulevard Saint-Germain, having got there a few minutes after Janvier."

"And Rougier?" asked Janvier, unable to keep from smiling at the comical side of it.

"He was standing in the middle of the sidewalk and saw me arrive. I pretended to be going somewhere in a hurry. He laughed at me and greeted me with: 'You looking for Janvier? He's just turned the corner of Rue Solférino.' It's always a pleasure to be made to feel like a fool by someone from the Rue des Saussaies. As it was impossible to get any information on Jacques Fleury in the neighborhood of the Ministry, I . . ."

"You looked for a telephone directory?" asked Janvier.

"I didn't think of it. I knew that he's a customer at the bars of the Champs-Elysées, so I went to Fouquet's."

"I bet he's in the directory."

"Possibly. Will you let me say what I've got to say?"

Janvier, by this time, was in a lightheaded teasing mood like someone who has just had a good scolding and is watching someone else being scolded in his turn.

In fact, all three of them, Maigret included, felt on foreign ground, each as awkward as the other, and each could imagine their colleagues at Criminal Investigation enjoying the joke behind their backs.

"I had a chat with the bartender. Fleury is notorious in a way. Most of the time he lives on credit as long as he can, and when he owes too much they don't allow him to be served any more. Then he disappears for a few days, until he has exhausted his credit in all the other bars and restaurants."

"Does he pay in the end?"

"He turns up eventually, in high spirits, and settles his account."

"And then it starts all over again?"

"Yes. It's been going on for years."

"Ever since he's been at the Ministry?"

"With the difference that now he is private secretary and people think he has some influence, more of them supply him with food and drink. Before that he used to disappear for months on end. One day he was seen working at the Halles, counting the cabbages coming off a truck."

Janvier darted a significant glance at Maigret.

"He has a wife and two children, somewhere in the direction of Vanves. He is supposed to be supporting them. Luckily, his wife has a job, something like housekeeping for an elderly gentleman. The children work, too."

"Whom does he go to the bars with?"

"For a long time it was with a woman of about forty, a stout woman with dark hair, they tell me, known as Marcelle; he seemed to be in love with her. Some say that he picked her up when she was a cashier at a brasserie at Porte Saint-Martin. Nobody knows what became of her. For more than a year he has been seen with a Jacqueline Page and lives with her in an apartment on Rue Washington, above an Italian grocer's. Jacqueline Page is twenty-three years old and sometimes works as an extra in movies. She cultivates all the producers, directors, and actors who come to Fouquet's and is as accommodating as they could wish."

"Is Fleury in love with her?"

"Apparently."

"Is he jealous?"

"So they say. But he doesn't dare protest and pretends not to notice anything."

"Have you seen her?"

"I thought I ought to go to Rue Washington."

"What sort of story did you tell her?"

"There was no need of a story. As soon as she opened her door, she exclaimed: 'What, another one?' "

Janvier and Maigret could not help exchanging a smile.

"Another what?" asked Maigret, knowing perfectly well what the reply would be.

"Another policeman, you know what I mean. Two of them had been there before me."

"Separately?"

"No, together."

"Did they question her about Fleury?"

"They asked her if he worked in the evenings and brought documents home from the Ministry."

"What did she tell them?"

"That they had better things to do with their evenings. That girl doesn't mince her words. Curiously enough, her mother looks after the pews in the church at Picpus."

"Did they search the apartment?"

"No, they just had a look at the rooms. It isn't really an apartment. It's more like a camping site. The kitchen's just large enough to prepare breakfast in. The other rooms, a living room, a bedroom, and what could be called a dining room, were in complete chaos, with shoes and a woman's underclothes all over the place and records and magazines, paperbacks, not counting the bottles and glasses."

"Does he go home for lunch?"

"Rarely. Usually she stays in bed until the middle of the afternoon. Now and then he calls her up in the morning proposing that she meet him in a restaurant."

"Have they got many friends?"

"Just people who go to the same dives as they do."

"Is that all?"

For the first time, Lucas's voice rang with an almost pathetic reproach as he answered:

"No, it isn't! Your instructions were to provide you with as much information as possible. In the first place I have here a list of about a dozen of Jacqueline's former lovers, including some that she still goes on seeing."

With an expression of disgust, he threw a paper with penciled names on it on the table.

"You'll see that it has the names of two politicians. Another thing: I almost rediscovered the girl Marcelle."

"How did you do that?"

"On my two legs. I toured the bars of the main boulevards, beginning with the one by the Opéra. As usual, it was the last one, on Place de la République, that was the right one."

"Marcelle has gone back to being a cashier?"

"No, but they remember her and have seen her in the neighborhood. The owner of the bar believes that she lives in the vicinity, in the direction of Rue Blondel. He has met her often on Rue de Croissant, so he supposes that she works in a newspaper office or in a printing house."

"Did you check?"

"Not yet. Do I have to?"

The tone was such that Maigret murmured:

"Angry?"

Lucas forced himself to smile.

"No. But you must admit it's a crazy sort of job. Especially when one learns afterward from the paper that it's this wretched business we're on to! If I have to go on, I'll go on. But I can tell you frankly . . ."

"You think I'm not as fed up as you are?"

"No. I know you are."

"Rue de Croissant is not as long as all that. Everyone knows everyone else in that part of the world."

"And I suppose I'll get there just after the boys of the Rue des Saussaies, like last time!"

"It's very probable."

"All right, I'll go. May I have another?" He was pointing to his glass, which he had just emptied. Maigret gave a sign to the waiter to repeat the order and at the last moment ordered himself a Pernod instead of a beer.

Inspectors from other departments had come to have a drink at the bar at the end of the day and waved their hands in greeting. Maigret was frowning, thinking of Auguste Point, who must have read the article and must be expecting to see his own name in equally large letters in the papers any minute now. His wife, whom he must have informed of the whole business, was probably as anxious as he was. Had he spoken to Mademoiselle Blanche? Did they realize, the three of them, just how much activity was going on around them?

"What am I to do now?" asked Janvier in the tone of one repelled by his assignment, but resigned to seeing it through.

"Are you game enough to keep watch on Rue Vaneau?"

"For the whole night?"

"No. I'll send Torrence to relieve you at about eleven, let's say."

"You think something will happen there?"

Maigret admitted:

"No."

He had not the vaguest idea. Or rather he had so

many and such muddled ideas that he could not make head or tail of them. One had to come back to the simpler facts, those one could control. It was certain that on Monday afternoon the man Piquemal had gone to see the Minister of Public Works. He must have approached the usher, filled in a form. Maigret had not seen it, but it must have been put on record. Auguste Point could not have invented such a visit.

At least two persons from the adjoining offices were likely to have heard the conversation: Mademoiselle Blanche and Jacques Fleury.

Criminal Investigation had thought of that, too, as they had made inquiries at their lodgings.

Auguste Point had gone to his private place, on Boulevard Pasteur. He had locked the document in his desk. The Superintendent believed that this was true. Therefore, the person who had gone to see Mademoiselle Blanche the next morning and searched her apartment was not certain exactly where the report was to be found.

And in the afternoon the document had disappeared.

Wednesday morning Piquemal disappeared, too.

On the same day Joseph Mascoulin's paper first mentioned the Calame report and demanded publicly to know where the document was hidden.

Maigret's lips were moving; he spoke in a low voice, as though to himself.

"It's either one thing or the other: they may have stolen the report to destroy it, or they may have stolen it to use it. Up to now it seems that no one has used it."

Lucas and Janvier listened without interrupting him.

"Unless . . ."

Slowly he drank half of his glass, then wiped his mouth.

"It seems complicated, but when it's a question of politics, things are rarely simple. Only one or two people involved in the Clairfond case have any reason to destroy the document. If we learn that it has disappeared after having surfaced for a few hours, suspicion will automatically fall on them."

"I think I begin to understand," murmured Janvier.

"In this case, about thirty politicians at least, without counting Nicoud himself, are faced with a scandal and worse. If one succeeds in throwing suspicion on one individual and if one can produce evidence against him, this individual being vulnerable—one has the ideal scapegoat. Auguste Point's position is indefensible."

His two colleagues glanced at him in surprise. Maigret had forgotten that they knew only a part of the case. The point at which it was possible to keep things secret from them had been passed.

"He is on the list of Nicoud's guests at Samois," he told them. "The contractor made his daughter a present of a gold fountain pen."

"You saw it?"

He nodded.

"And it was he who . . . ?"

Lucas did not finish his question. Maigret had understood it. The inspector had wanted to say:

"It was he who asked you to help him?"

This at last dissipated the embarrassment that had weighed on the three men.

"Yes, it was. By now, I would be surprised if others didn't know it, too."

"Need we be secretive any more?"

"Certainly not as far as Criminal Investigation is concerned."

They lingered another quarter of an hour over their glasses. Maigret was the first to get up, wish them good night, and go to his office in case he was wanted. There was no message for him. Point had not telephoned, nor had anyone else connected with the Clairfond case.

At dinner Madame Maigret saw by his face that he had better not be questioned. He spent the evening reading a review of international police work and went to bed at ten.

"You have a lot of work at the moment?"

They were both ready for sleep. She had kept the question for a long time on the tip of her tongue.

"Not much, but what there is is nasty."

Twice, before falling asleep, he was tempted to call up Auguste Point. He did not know what he would have said to him, but he would have liked to establish contact.

At eight o'clock he was up. Behind the curtains, a light mist clung to the windowpanes and seemed to have muffled the noises of the street. He walked to the corner of Boulevard Richard-Lenoir to take the bus and stopped to buy the newspapers.

The bomb had exploded. The papers posed no more questions, but announced in headlines:

THE CLAIRFOND CASE

Disappearance of Jules Piquemal, who found the Calame report

The report which was handed in at a very high level is understood to have also disappeared.

His newspapers under his arm, he got into the bus and did not read any more before arriving at the Quai des Orfèvres.

As he walked down the hallway he heard the telephone ringing in his office, and hurried to pick up the receiver.

"Superintendent Maigret?" the operator asked. "It's the third time in a quarter of an hour that you have been called from the Ministry of Public Works. I'm putting you through now."

He still had his hat on and was still wearing his coat, which was slightly damp from the morning fog.

5

The voice was that of a man who had not slept the night before, had not slept the preceding nights, either, and who made no effort to choose his words because he had passed the stage of worrying about what he sounded like. It was that flat, lifeless, disheartened tone that, in a man, is the same as when a woman weeps in a certain way, her mouth wide open, and looks ugly without minding it.

"Can you come and see me at once, Maigret? Unless it embarrasses you personally, there is no reason now to avoid Boulevard Saint-Germain. I warn you that the waiting room is full of journalists and the telephone never stops. I have promised them a press conference at eleven o'clock."

Maigret glanced at his watch.

"I'll come right away."

There was a knock at the door. Lapointe walked in as Maigret was still holding the receiver, frowning deeply.

"You've got something to tell me?"

"Yes, some fresh news."

"Important?"

"I think so."

"Put on your hat and come with me. We can talk on the way."

He stopped for a moment at the door to ask the doorman to warn the boss that he would not be at the morning briefing. In the car park he went to one of the small black cars of Police Headquarters.

"You drive."

And as they were driving along the embankment:

"What have you got to tell me?"

"I spent the night at the Hôtel du Berry in the room I engaged."

"Piquemal hasn't reappeared?"

"No. A man from Criminal Investigation kept watch all night in the street."

Maigret was prepared for this. It was not disturbing.

"I didn't want to go to Piquemal's room while it was dark, for I'd have had to switch on the light and it would have been seen from the street. I waited till it was light and then gave it a more thorough search than I did the first time. I went through all the books one after the other and searched between the pages. In a treatise on political economy I found this letter, which had been slipped in as a bookmark."

Driving with one hand, he pulled his wallet out of his pocket with the other and passed it to Maigret.

"On the left side. The letter that's headed Chamber of Deputies."

It was a small note, like those the deputies use for short memoranda. It was dated the previous Thursday. The writing was small, uneven, with letters climbing one on top of the other and the ends of the words almost indecipherable.

Dear Sir,

I thank you for your communication. I am greatly interested in what you tell me and will be glad to see you tomorrow, toward eight in the evening at the Brasserie du Croissant, Rue Montmartre. I beg you not to mention the matter in question to anybody until then.

Yours

There was no real signature, simply a scrawl that might have meant anything.

"I suppose it's Joseph Mascoulin," growled the Superintendent.

"Yes, it's he. I went earlier to a friend who is a stenographer in the Chamber and knows most of the deputies' handwriting. I had only to show him the first line and the scrawl at the end."

They were already on Boulevard Saint-Germain, opposite the Ministry of Public Works. Maigret could recognize several cars belonging to the press. He glanced at the opposite sidewalk, but saw no one from the Rue des Saussaies. Now that the bomb had actually exploded, had they called off the watch?

"Do I wait for you?"

"Yes, that would be best."

He crossed the courtyard, went up the main stairs, and

found himself in a waiting room with a dark-red carpet and yellow columns. He recognized a few faces here and there. Two or three journalists were trying to approach him but an usher forestalled them.

"Will you come this way, Superintendent. The Minister is expecting you."

Auguste Point was standing waiting for Maigret in the huge dark study, with all its lamps lit, and seemed to him stouter and more massive than in the Boulevard Pasteur apartment. He shook Maigret's hand, held it for an instant in his own, with the pressure of one who has just sustained a great shock and is grateful for the slightest display of sympathy.

"Thank you for coming, Maigret. I cannot help reproaching myself now for involving you in all this. You can see that I was right to be anxious."

He turned to a middle-aged woman who had been telephoning and had put down the receiver.

"May I introduce Mademoiselle Blanche, my secretary, whom I mentioned to you."

Mademoiselle Blanche glanced suspiciously at Maigret, very much on the defensive. She did not stretch out her hand, but merely nodded in his direction.

Her face was undistinguished, not attractive, but under her simple black dress, brightened only by a narrow strip of white lace at the neck, Maigret was aware with surprise of a body still young and rounded and very desirable.

"If you don't mind, we'll go to my apartment. I've never been able to get used to this office; I never feel at ease in it. You'll take all the calls, Blanche, won't you?"

"Yes, Your Excellency."

Auguste Point opened the door at the back and murmured, in the same flat voice:

"I'll go first. It's rather complicated getting there."

He himself was not quite sure of the way and seemed lost in the deserted corridors, where he hesitated before several doors.

They came to a narrow staircase, went up, and walked through two large empty rooms. A servant in a white apron, holding a broom, passed them, which indicated that they had reached the private apartments.

"I meant to introduce Fleury to you. He was in the office next door. At the last moment I forgot about it."

Now they could hear the sound of a woman's voice. Point pushed open another door and they were in a small living room where a woman was sitting by the window with a young woman beside her.

"My wife and daughter. I considered it right to talk in their presence."

Madame Point could have been any little middle-aged bourgeoise whom one meets shopping in the street. Her face, too, looked tense, her eyes a little vacant.

"I must tell you right away how grateful I am to you, Superintendent. My husband has told me everything, and I know how much the conversation he had with you has helped him."

Newspapers, with sensational headlines, were spread out on the table.

At first Maigret paid slight attention to the young woman, who seemed calmer, more controlled, than either of her parents.

"Would you like a cup of coffee?"

It all reminded him a little of a house where someone

has just died, and the daily routine is suddenly interrupted, and people are coming and going and bustling about without knowing where to settle or what to do. He still had his overcoat on. Anne-Marie asked him to take it off and hung it over an armchair.

"Have you read this morning's papers?" the Minister asked at last, still standing.

"I only had time to look at the headlines."

"They don't mention my name yet, but all of the Press know about it. They must have got their information in the middle of the night. I was told so by a typesetter on Rue du Croissant. I immediately telephoned the President."

"What was his reaction?"

"I don't know whether he was surprised or not. I've lost my capacity of judging people's reactions. Obviously I was interrupting his sleep. It seemed to me that he showed some astonishment, but I found as I talked to him on the telephone that he was less disturbed than I had expected him to be."

He appeared to be talking in a forced manner, without any conviction, as though words no longer had any importance.

"Sit down, Maigret. I apologize for standing all the time, but I haven't been able to make myself sit down since this morning. It's driving me mad. I've got to keep standing and walking up and down. Before you came in I had been pacing in my office for an hour while my secretary was answering the telephone. Where was I? Oh, yes. The President said something like: 'Well, my friend, we'll have to face the music!' I believe those were his exact words. I asked him if it was his men who were detaining Piquemal. Instead of answering me directly he muttered something like: 'What makes you think that?' Then he explained to me that he couldn't swear to what was going on in his departments any more than I or any other Minister could. He gave me a lecture on the subject: 'We are made responsible for everything,' he was saying, 'though in fact we're only passing through and the people we give orders to know perfectly well they had a different boss yesterday and may well have a different one tomorrow.' I suggested that the best I could do was to offer him my resignation the next morning.

" 'You're too hasty, Point,' he said. 'In politics, things don't happen as they're expected to happen. I'll think your suggestion over and call you up shortly.'

"I suppose that he telephoned some of our colleagues. Perhaps they met to discuss the matter. I don't know. At the moment they have no reason to keep me informed.

"I spent the rest of the night pacing up and down in my room, with my wife trying to reason with me."

Point's wife looked at Maigret as though trying to say: "Help me! You see what a state he is in!"

It was true. That earlier evening on Boulevard Pasteur, Point had seemed to Maigret like a man staggering under a sudden blow and incapable of dealing with it but prepared to put up a good fight. Now he spoke as though he was no longer concerned with events, as though he had given up, knowing his destiny had been taken out of his hands.

"Did he call you back?" asked Maigret.

"At about half past five. As you see, there were quite a number of us awake last night. He said that my resignation would serve no useful purpose, that it would only be considered an admission of guilt, and that all I had to do was to tell the truth."

"Including the contents of the Calame report?" asked the Superintendent.

Point managed a smile.

"No. Not exactly. Just when I believed the conversation had come to an end he added: 'I daresay you'll be asked whether you have read the report.' I replied: 'I *have* read it.'

" 'That's what I had understood. It's a very lengthy report, filled, I presume, with technical details on a subject not necessarily familiar to a legal mind. It might be more exact to say that you had skimmed through it. You haven't got it to hand at the moment to refresh your memory. The reason I am saying this, my friend, is to help you avoid more serious difficulties than those you have to face already. If you speak of the contents of the report and implicate anyone, whoever it may be—it doesn't concern me and I don't care one way or the other—you'll be accused of making charges which you are unable to support. Do you understand me?' "

For at least the third time since the beginning of the conversation Point lit his pipe, and his wife turned to Maigret.

"Do smoke, if you wish. I'm used to it."

"From seven o'clock on the telephone never stopped ringing—mostly journalists wanting to question me. At first I told them that I had no announcement to make. Then they almost seemed to be threatening me. Two newspaper editors called me personally. In the end I asked everybody to come to my office at eleven o'clock today, for a press conference. I had to see you beforehand. I suppose that . . ."

He had had the courage, perhaps through tact, or fear, or even superstition, to wait until now to put the question.

"I suppose you haven't discovered anything?"

Perhaps it was on purpose, to make the gesture more significant and thus inspire confidence in the Minister, but when he pulled the letter from his pocket and handed it to Auguste Point he did it in complete silence. There was something theatrical about it, which was out of character.

Madame Point did not move from the sofa where she was sitting, but Anne-Marie went up to her father and read over his shoulder.

"Who is it from?" she asked.

Maigret in his turn was asking Point:

"Do you recognize the handwriting?"

"It seems familiar, but I can't quite place it."

"This letter was sent last Thursday by Joseph Mascoulin."

"To whom?"

"To Julien Piquemal."

There was a silence. Point, without a word, handed the note to his wife. Each of them was trying to assess the importance of this discovery.

When Maigret began to speak again it was, as at Boulevard Pasteur, in the form of an interrogation.

"What sort of terms are you on with Mascoulin?"

"No terms at all."

"Have you quarreled?"

"No."

Point looked grave, preoccupied. Maigret, although he never meddled in politics, was not quite ignorant of parliamentary custom. In a general way, the deputies, even though belonging to different parties, and even though attacking one another ferociously in the political forum, could still maintain friendly relationships with one another, reminiscent, in their familiarity, of relationships in schools and barracks.

"You are not on speaking terms?" Maigret insisted.

Point drew his hand across his forehead.

"All this goes back a few years, to my first days in the Chamber. A bright new Chamber, as you probably remember, and we all swore we would keep out anyone whose hands weren't clean. It was immediately after the war, and the country was swept by a wave of idealism, a thirst for decency. The majority of my colleagues, at any rate a large number of them, were as new to politics as I was."

"Not Mascoulin."

"No. There were a few left from the old Chamber, but everyone was convinced that the newcomers would create the right atmosphere. After a few months I was not quite so confident. After two years I was discouraged. You remember, Henriette?"

He turned to his wife.

"It got to the point," she said, "where he had decided not to run again."

"At a dinner at which I had to speak I expressed my misgivings in so many words, and the press was there to put it all on record. I should be very much surprised if they don't remind me of some parts of my speech any day now. The subject of it was dirty hands. I tried to explain that basically it was not our political machine that was deficient, but the climate in which politicians have to live, whether they like it or not. I needn't repeat it all now. You remember the famous slogan: 'The Republic of Comrades.' We meet every day. We shake hands like old friends. After a few weeks everybody is on familiar terms and each man tries to help the next. As the days go by, you shake more and more hands, and if these are not quite clean you shrug tolerantly and say: 'Oh, well, he's not a bad guy,' or 'He has to do it to keep his votes.' You follow me? I had stated publicly that if each of us refused once and for all to shake dirty hands, the hands of any individual not quite straight, the political atmosphere would be purified immediately."

After a few moments he added bitterly:

"I practiced what I preached. I avoided certain journalists and unsavory businessmen who haunt the corridors of the Palais Bourbon. I refused certain services to some influential electors which I believed I ought to refuse. And one day Mascoulin came up to me, his hand outstretched. I pretended not to see him and turned very ostentatiously toward another colleague. I know he went scarlet in the face and has never forgiven me. He is the kind of man who doesn't forgive."

"You did something like that with Hector Tabard, the editor of the *Rumor*, didn't you?"

"I refused to see him a couple of times, and he didn't insist."

He glanced at his watch.

"I have only one hour left, Maigret. At eleven o'clock

I'll have to face the journalists and answer their questions. I had thought of handing them a statement, but it wouldn't satisfy them. I've got to tell them that Piquemal came to me with the Calame report and that I went to my apartment on Boulevard Pasteur to read it."

"And that you didn't do so?"

"I will try to be less explicit. The most difficult, the impossible part will be to get them to accept my leaving the famous report in an apartment without any supervision, and that when the next day I wanted to pick it up to take it to the President of the Council it had disappeared. Nobody will believe me. Piquemal's disappearance doesn't simplify anything—quite the contrary. They will say that it was one way of shutting up an embarrassing witness. The only thing that could have saved me would have been to present them with the thief."

He added, as though apologizing for his resentment:

"I couldn't have expected that in forty-eight hours, even from you. What do you think I should do?"

Madame Point interrupted with determination.

"Hand in your resignation and we'll go back to La Roche-sur-Yon. The people who know you will know you are not guilty. You don't have to worry about the others. Your conscience is clear, isn't it?"

Maigret's eyes turned to Anne-Marie, and he saw her purse her lips. He realized that the young woman did not share her mother's views and that as far as she was concerned such a retreat on her father's part would mean that she would have to give up all her hopes.

"What is your opinion?" Point murmured, hesitantly.

This was a responsibility the Superintendent could not accept.

"And what is yours?"

"I feel I ought to hold out, at least if there's even the slightest hope of finding the thief."

It was once again an indirect question.

"I keep on hoping, right up to the last minute," grumbled Maigret, "otherwise I would never take on a case in the first place. Because I'm on foreign ground with politics, I lost some time in activities that may appear useless. But I'm not at all sure that they are as useless as they seem."

Maigret had to instill some assurance in Point, if not a certain confidence, before he met the journalists, so he began to go over the situation, clarifying it.

"You see, Your Excellency, we have arrived at a point where I feel more at home. Until now I've had to work by stealth, as it were, though in fact we've bumped into the men from Rue des Saussaies all along the line. No matter where we went, the men from Criminal Investigation were always there—at the door of your Ministry, at your secretary's lodgings, at Piquemal's, or at your parliamentary private secretary's place. At one moment I wondered what they were looking for, and whether the two departments weren't perhaps pursuing parallel inquiries. Now I am inclined to believe that all they wanted was to see what we discovered. It wasn't you, or your secretary, or Piquemal, or Fleury who was being watched, it was me and my men. Once Piquemal's disappearance and the disappearance of the documents became official, then Criminal Investigation could call off their watch as it automatically became the business of Police Headquarters anyway, being within the jurisdiction of Paris. A man doesn't disappear without leaving a trace. And a thief is always caught in the end."

"Sooner or later . . ." murmured Point with a sad smile.

Maigret got up and looked him straight in the eyes:

"It's your job to hold out until then."

"It doesn't depend only on me."

"It depends mostly on you."

"If Mascoulin is behind this maneuver he will challenge the government quite soon."

"Unless he prefers to profit from what he knows to increase his influence."

Point glanced at him with surprise.

"You know so much? I thought you knew very little of politics."

"This kind of thing doesn't happen only in politics; there are Mascoulins in every walk of life. I believe—tell me if I'm wrong—that he has one passion only, a passion for power, but he is a cold-blooded animal who knows how to bide his time. Every now and then he opens fire in the Chamber or in the press by uncovering some kind of scandal or misuse of authority."

Point was listening with renewed interest.

"Little by little, in this way he has created for himself a reputation as a merciless crusader. So that all the fanatics, the embittered, the rebels of Piquemal's type go to him as soon as they think they have uncovered something dubious. I'm sure he must receive the same sort of letters as we do when some mysterious crime is committed. We get letters from madmen, cranks and maniacs, and from people who snatch the opportunity to indulge their hatred for a relative, or some old friend or neighbor. Among them there are always some who provide us with real evidence, without which a good many murderers would still be loose on the streets. Piquemal the hermit, the seeker after truth in all extremist parties, in religion, in philosophy—he's precisely the kind of man who, when he found the Calame report, would never for a moment have considered handing it over to his immediate superiors, whom he doesn't trust. He turned to the professional crusader, convinced that, by doing so, the report would escape God knows what secret conspiracy."

"If Mascoulin has the report, why hasn't he used it yet?"

"For the reason I have just given you. He must, periodically, launch a scandal in order to keep up his reputation. But neither he nor such blackmailing sheets as the *Rumor* publish all the information they get. Rather, it's the things they keep silent about that are the most profitable: the Calame report is too precious a morsel to throw to the common herd. If Mascoulin has it in his possession, how many top people do you reckon he has at his mercy, including Arthur Nicoud?"

"Quite a number. Several dozen."

"We don't know how many Calame reports he holds, which he can use at any moment and which will allow him to achieve his aims, the day he feels in a strong enough position."

"I had thought of that," Point admitted. "And it's that that frightens me. If it's Mascoulin who's keeping the report back it is perfectly safe and I would be surprised if it ever turned up. And if we don't produce it or if we have no formal proof that a certain person has destroyed it, I will be dishonored because it is I who will be accused of causing it to disappear."

Maigret saw Madame Point turn her head away because a tear was running down her cheek. Point saw it, too, and for a moment was almost overcome himself, while Anne-Marie was saying:

"Mama!"

Madame Point shook her head as if to indicate it was nothing and left the room abruptly.

"You see!" her husband said, as though the incident needed no comment.

Was Maigret injudicious in allowing himself to be influenced by the dramatic atmosphere around him and to declare, with complete assurance:

"I can't promise you to find the report, but I'll be damned if I don't put my hand on the man or woman who got into your apartment and stole it. That at least is my profession."

"You think you can?"

"I'm sure of it."

He had risen from his chair. Point murmured:

"I'll take you down."

And turning to his daughter:

"Run and tell your mother what the Superintendent has just said to me. It will do her good."

They went back the same way as they had come through the maze of the Ministry and found themselves once again in Point's office, where, beside Mademoiselle Blanche, who was answering the telephone, a tall, slender man, with gray hair, stood sorting the mail.

"I would like to introduce Jacques Fleury, my parliamentary private secretary . . . Superintendent Maigret."

Maigret thought that he had seen the man somewhere before, probably in a bar or a restaurant. He carried himself well and was dressed with a certain elegance, in striking contrast to the careless attire of the Minister. He was the type one frequently meets in the bars of the Champs-Elysées in the company of pretty women.

His hand was dry, his handshake frank. He looked younger, more energetic, from a distance; close to, one saw the weary pouches under the eyes, the slight droop of the lips which he concealed by a nervous smile.

"How many are there?" Point asked him, pointing to the waiting room.

"A good thirty. There are some correspondents from foreign papers as well. I don't know how many camera men, they've been coming in steadily."

Maigret and the Minister exchanged glances. Maigret seemed to be saying with an encouraging wink:

"Keep your chin up!"

Point asked him:

"Will you go out through the waiting room?"

"Since you will be telling them that I'm in charge of the inquiry, it no longer matters. Quite the contrary."

He was aware all the time of the suspicious glances of Mademoiselle Blanche; he had not had time to win her over. She seemed to be hesitant as to how to judge him. Maybe the composure of her employer convinced her, however, that Maigret's intervention was a good thing.

When the Superintendent went through the waiting

room the photographers were the first to rush toward him, and he did nothing to avoid them. The reporters, too, showered him with questions.

"Are you interested in the Calame report?"

He waved them away with a smile.

"In a few minutes the Minister himself will answer your questions."

"You're not denying that you are connected with it?"

"I deny nothing."

Some of them followed him to the marble staircase, hoping to force a statement out of him.

"Ask the Minister," he repeated.

One of them asked: "D'you believe that Piquemal has been murdered?"

It was the first time that this hypothesis had been clearly formulated.

"You know my favorite answer," he replied: "I believe nothing."

A few moments later, after further attempts from the photographers, he got into the car where Lapointe was waiting, having spent his time reading the newspapers.

""Where are we going? To the Quai?"

"No. Boulevard Pasteur. What do the papers say?"

"Mostly they're preoccupied with Piquemal's disappearance. One of them, I don't remember which, went to interview Madame Calame, who is still in the apartment where she lived with her husband, Boulevard Raspail. She seems to be an energetic little woman who doesn't mince her words and didn't try to avoid questions. She hadn't read the report, but she remembers well that her husband went to spend a few weeks in the

Haute-Savoie, about five years ago. On his return he was very busy, and it often happened that he worked till late at night.

"Never before had he had so many telephone calls, she said. Crowds of people came to see him, whom we didn't know from Adam. He was anxious and preoccupied. When I asked him what was worrying him, he told me it was his work and responsibilities. He often spoke of responsibilities at that time. I had the impression that something was gnawing at him. I knew he was ill. Over a year before the doctor had told me that he was suffering from cancer. I remember that once he sighed: 'Good God, how difficult it is to know where one's duty lies!' "

They were driving down Rue Vaugirard, and a bus was hampering their progress.

"There's a whole column about it," added Lapointe.

"What did she do with her husband's papers?"

"She left them all as they were in his study, which she cleans regularly, just as she did when he was alive."

"Had anybody come to see her recently?"

"Two people," replied Lapointe, with an admiring glance at his boss.

"Piquemal?"

"Yes. That was the first visit, about a week ago."

"Did she know him?"

"She didn't know him well. While Calame was alive, he often came to get advice from him. She thinks he was studying mathematics. He explained that he wanted to find one of his papers he had once given to his teacher."

"Did he find it?"

"He had a brief case with him. She left him in the study, where he remained about an hour. When he came out, she asked him if he had found what he wanted and he said no, that unfortunately his paper must have been lost. She didn't look in his brief case. She had no suspicions. It was only two days after . . ."

"Who was the second visitor?"

"A man of about forty, who pretended to be a former pupil of Calame's and asked her if she had kept Calame's files. He, too, talked of some work that they had done together."

"Did she allow him into the study?"

"No. She thought the coincidence was too strange and replied that all her husband's papers had been left in the School of Engineering."

"Did she describe her second visitor?"

"The paper doesn't mention it. If she did the reporter is keeping it to himself and is probably pursuing his own little inquiry."

"Park here, by this sidewalk. We're here."

By day the boulevard was as peaceful as by night, with its own particular reassuring character of middle-class life.

"Do I wait for you?"

"You'll come with me. We'll probably have some work to do."

The concierge's glass door was on the left of the hall. She was an elderly, rather dignified woman, and obviously tired.

"What is it?" she asked the two men, without getting out of her armchair, while a russet-colored cat jumped from her lap and came to rub itself against Maigret's legs. The latter gave his name, took off his hat, and was careful to give his words a respectful note.

"Monsieur Point has asked me to make inquiries about a robbery of which he was a victim two days ago."

"A robbery? In the house? He never said anything to me about it!"

"He will confirm it to you when he sees you, and if you have any doubts about it all you have to do is telephone him."

"That's all right. If you're the Superintendent, I've got to believe what you say, haven't I? But how could it have happened? This is a quiet house. The police haven't had to set foot in it for the thirty-five years I've been here."

"I would like you to try to remember what happened on Tuesday, particularly in the morning."

"Tuesday . . . Wait a moment . . . That was the day before yesterday."

"Yes. The Minister came to his apartment that evening."

"Did he tell you that?"

"Not only did he tell me, but I met him there. You opened the door automatically for me a little after ten o'clock."

"I think I remember, yes."

"He must have left a short time after me."

"Yes."

"Did you open the door to anyone else that night?"

"Certainly not. It's rare that the tenants come home later than midnight. They are all quiet people. I would have remembered if I had."

"When do you open the door in the morning?"

"At half past six, sometimes seven."

"After that you remain in the lodge?"

It consisted of one room, with a gas stove, a round table, a sink, and, behind the curtain, a bed with a dark-red cover.

"Except when I sweep the stairs."

"What time is that?"

"Not before nine. After that, I distribute the mail, which comes at half past eight."

"The elevator has glass walls, so I suppose you can see who goes up and down?"

"Yes. I always watch it, it's a habit."

"Did you see someone going up to the fourth floor that morning?"

"I'm certain I didn't."

"Nobody asked you if the Minister was at home that morning or even early in the afternoon?"

"Nobody. There was only a telephone call."

"To you?"

"No, to the apartment."

"How do you happen to know?"

"Because I was on the stairs between the fourth and fifth floors."

"What time was it?"

"Perhaps ten o'clock. Perhaps a little earlier. My feet don't let me work quickly any more. I heard the telephone behind the door. It rang for a long time. Then, a quarter of an hour later, when I'd finished cleaning and came down there was the telephone again, and I remember I said to myself 'You can ring as long as you like.' "

"And then?"

"Nothing."

"You went back to the lodge?"

"To tidy myself up a bit."

"You didn't leave the house?"

"For about a quarter of an hour or twenty minutes, as I do every morning, just for my marketing. The grocer is next door, the butcher's at the corner. From the grocer's I can see who comes and goes. I always keep an eye on the house."

"And from the butcher's?"

"I can't see, but I'm never there very long. I live alone with my cat and buy the same thing almost every day. At my age, you don't have much of an appetite."

"You don't know exactly what time it was when you were at the butcher's?"

"Not precisely. There is one of those great big clocks over the cashier's desk, but I never look at it."

"When you got back, you saw no one leave that you hadn't seen come in?"

"I don't remember. No. I'm more concerned with the ones that come in than with the ones that go out, apart from the tenants, that is, because with them I have to be able to answer whether they're in or not. There are always the tradesmen, the gas men, and the vacuum-cleaner salesmen."

He knew that he would get nothing more from her and that if, later on, she remembered some detail, she would be sure to let him know.

"The inspector and I are going to question your tenants," said Maigret.

"Go ahead. You'll see they're all decent people, except perhaps the old woman on the third, who . . ."

Maigret felt much more himself now he was back on a routine job again.

"We'll come to see you before we leave," he promised.

And he took care before he left to stroke the cat.

"You take the apartments on the left," he said to Lapointe, "and I'll tackle the ones on the right. You understand what I'm looking for?"

And he added, familiarly:

"Go to it, old boy!"

6

Before ringing at the first door Maigret hesitated and turned to Lapointe, who, on his side, had his finger on the bell.

"You're not thirsty?"

"No, Chief."

"You start. I'll be back in a moment."

At a pinch he might have made the telephone call he had suddenly thought of from the concierge's lodge. But apart from the fact that he preferred to talk without witnesses, he felt it would be good to have a drink at this stage—a glass of white wine, for instance. He had to go about a hundred yards before he found a small bar with not a soul inside besides the owner.

"A glass of white wine," he ordered.

He changed his mind.

"No, I'll have a Pernod."

It fitted better with his mood and with the time of day, also with this tidy little bar, which seemed permanently empty. He waited to be served and had emptied half of his glass before he went to the telephone.

When the newspapers report the story of an investigation, the impression is that the police follow through on a straight line, that they know where they are going from the start. Events follow one another with necessary logic, like the entries and exits of characters in a well-directed play.

Unnecessary comings and goings are rarely mentioned, and neither are the tedious searches in various directions that turn out to be red herrings.

Maigret could not have mentioned a single investigation during which, at one moment or the other, he had not floundered. This morning he had not had the time, at Police Headquarters, to question Lucas, Janvier, and Torrence, who had all been given instructions the day before, all of which this morning seemed of no importance.

"Police Headquarters? Get Lucas on the line, please. If he isn't there, give me Janvier."

He heard Lucas's voice at the other end.

"Is that you, Chief?"

"It is. First of all, will you make a note of something very urgent. I want you to get hold of a photograph of Piquemal, the guy from the School of Engineering. It's useless to look for one in his hotel room. I'd be surprised if they haven't one of those group photos at the school, the kind they take usually at the end of the year. The men at the Criminal Records Office may find it useful. I want them to get on to it as quickly as possible. There's still time to get the photo into the afternoon papers. It is to be transmitted to all police stations too. To be sure to miss nothing, I want inquiries made at the Medico-Legal Institute."

"Okay, Chief."

"Anything to report?"

"I've found the woman called Marcelle; her name is Marcelle Luquet."

In his own mind Maigret had already abandoned this line of inquiry, but he did not want to make Lucas feel he had worked for nothing.

"And?"

"She works as a proofreader at the Imprimerie du Croissant; she's on the night shift there. It isn't where they print the *Rumor* or the *Globe*. She's heard Tabard mentioned, but doesn't know him personally. She has never met Mascoulin."

"Did you talk to her?"

"I offered her a cup of coffee at Rue Montmartre. She's a nice woman. She lived alone until she met Fleury and fell in love with him. She still loves him. She bears him no grudge for leaving her, and if he'd have her back to-morrow she'd go back to him like a shot. According to her, he's just a great child who needs understanding and affection. She insists that though he may be capable of childish maneuvering, he is incapable of real dishonesty."

"Is Janvier around?"

"Yes."

"Put him on, will you."

Janvier had nothing to report. He had walked the

street in front of the apartment house on Rue Vaneau, until Torrence came to relieve him.

"Blanche Lamotte came home on foot, alone, about eleven o'clock, and went up to her room, where the light was on for about half an hour."

"There was no one around from the Rue des Saussaies?"

"No one. I was able to count the people in the street, coming back from the movies or the theater. Torrence had had an even less eventful time. He had only seen seven people in Rue Vaneau the whole night. The light went on at six o'clock. I suppose she gets up early to do her chores. She went out at ten minutes past eight and walked in the direction of Boulevard Saint-Germain."

Maigret went back and finished his Pernod at the bar, and since it was a small one, he ordered another while he was filling his pipe.

When he went back to the house on Boulevard Pasteur he found that Lapointe was busy at his third apartment, and he began patiently to do his own stint. Questioning people can be a long-drawn-out affair. At this hour both men found only women at their chores. Their first reaction was to close the door on them, thinking they were peddling some kind of domestic gadget or were insurance agents. At the word "police," they all gave a start in exactly the same way. While the men talked to them, their minds were elsewhere, on what they had on the stove, or what the baby was up to on the floor, or the vacuum cleaner they had left running. Some of them were embarrassed at being caught in their working clothes and automatically tried to straighten their hair.

"Please try to remember what you did on Tuesday morning. . . ."

"Tuesday, yes . . ."

"Did you happen, for instance, to open your door between ten and twelve?"

The first woman whom Maigret questioned had not been home at the time but in the hospital, where her sister was having an operation. The second, quite a young woman, was holding a child on her arm, supporting it on her hip, and was constantly confusing Tuesday and Wednesday.

"I was here, yes. I'm always here in the morning. I do my marketing at the end of the afternoon, after my husband comes back."

"Did you happen to open your door?"

With infinite patience they had to be gradually led back to that Tuesday morning. Had they been asked point-blank: "Did you see, in the elevator or on the stairs, a stranger going up to the fourth floor?" they would confidently have replied "No" without giving themselves time to think.

At the third floor Maigret caught up with Lapointe, because he had found no one on his side of the second floor.

The tenants, in tune with the house, lived quiet uneventful domestic lives behind their doors. The smells varied from one floor to the other, as did the colors of the wallpaper, but it all belonged to the same honest, laborious type of people, the type that is always slightly intimidated by the police. Maigret was struggling with a deaf old woman who did not ask him in and made him repeat every question. He could hear Lapointe talking behind the door opposite.

"Why should I have opened my door?" cried the deaf woman. "Has that cat of a concierge accused me of spying on the tenants?"

"Certainly not, Madame. You aren't being accused of anything."

"Then why do the police come and question me?"

"We're trying to establish whether a man . . ."

"What man?"

"A man whom we don't know, but whom we're searching for."

"What are you searching for?"

"A man."

"What has he done?"

He was still trying to make her understand when the door opposite opened. Lapointe was signaling to Maigret that he had discovered something, and the Superintendent abruptly broke off negotiations with the irate old woman.

"This is Madame Gaudry, Chief. Her husband works in a bank on Boulevard des Italiens. She has a little boy of five."

Maigret could see the boy hiding behind his mother, clutching at her skirt.

"She sometimes sends the boy to get something in the neighborhood in the morning, but only if the shop is on this side of the boulevard."

"I don't allow him to cross the street. And I always keep the door half open when he is out. That is how on Tuesday . . ."

"You heard someone go up?"

"Yes. I was waiting for Bob. At one moment I thought it was him. Most people take the elevator, but I don't allow him to do that yet."

"I can easily work the elevator!" the boy affirmed. "I've done it already."

"And you got punished for it! What happened was, I just looked out at the very moment a man was crossing the landing and going up to the fourth floor."

"What time was it?"

"About half past ten. I had just put my stew on the stove."

"Did the man speak to you?"

"No. At first I only saw him from the back. He was wearing a light beige overcoat, perhaps it was a raincoat, I didn't look too close, and he had broad shoulders and a thick neck."

She glanced at Maigret's neck.

"Rather like mine?"

She hesitated, blushing.

"Not quite. He was younger than you are. In his forties, I would say. I could see his face when he got to the turn of the stairs, and he looked back at me and seemed upset to find me there."

"He stopped on the fourth floor?"

"Yes."

"Did he ring a bell?"

"No. He went into Monsieur Point's apartment; it took him quite a time to open the door."

"As though he were trying several keys?"

"I couldn't swear to that, but it was as if he wasn't familiar with the lock."

"Did you see him leave?"

"I didn't see him because coming down he took the elevator."

"Was he there for a long time?"

"Less than ten minutes."

"Did you stay on the landing all that time?"

"No. But Bob wasn't back yet and I left the door half open. I heard the elevator go up, stop at the fourth floor, and go down again."

"Could you describe him, apart from his stoutness?"

"It's not easy. He had a red complexion like a man who likes his food."

"Glasses?"

"I don't think so. In fact, I'm certain he didn't."

"Was he smoking a pipe? A cigarette?"

"No. . . . Wait a moment. . . . I'm almost certain he was smoking a cigar. . . . It struck me because my brother-in-law . . ."

All, including the cigar, fitted the description supplied by the bar owner on Rue Jacob of the man who had approached Piquemal. It would also have fitted the description of the stranger who had visited Mademoiselle Blanche on Rue Vaneau.

A few moments later Maigret and Lapointe met on the sidewalk.

"Where are we going?"

"Take me to the Quai. After that, you'll go to Rue Vaneau and Rue Jacob to find out if by any chance the man was smoking a cigar."

When Maigret got to his office he found that Lucas had already obtained a photograph in which Piquemal appeared, though unfortunately only in the background;

it was, however, clear enough for the specialists of the Criminal Records Office to work with.

He sent in his name to the Chief of Police and spent about half an hour explaining the developments.

"Well, at least we've got something to go on," sighed the Chief when Maigret had finished.

"Yes, that's something."

"I'll be even happier when we learn—if we ever do learn—who this man is."

Both had the same suspicion and preferred not to speak of it. It was not impossible that the individual, whose tracks they had discovered three times now, was someone belonging to the other Department, to Rue des Saussaies. Maigret had good friends there, especially a man called Catroux, to whose son he had been godfather. He hesitated to approach him, for if Catroux knew anything he risked putting him in an awkward position.

Piquemal's photograph would appear in the afternoon papers. It would be ironical if the man they were looking for had all the time been in the hands of the Criminal Investigation Department. They might have put him temporarily out of circulation because he knew too much. Perhaps they had taken him to the Rue des Saussaies to pump him? The papers were going to announce that the Police and Maigret in particular were in charge of the case. It would be fair play for Criminal Investigation to let him loose in the country, then a few hours later to announce that they had found Piquemal.

'You do believe, of course," insisted the Chief, "that Point is an honest man and is not concealing anything from you?"

"I could swear to it."

"And the people round him?"

"I've made inquiries about each one of them. I don't know everything about their lives, of course, but what I do know makes me think that we must look elsewhere. The letter I showed you . . ."

"Mascoulin?"

"He's certainly mixed up in this business. The letter proves it."

"What are you going to do?"

"Maybe it won't get me very far, but for some reason I'd like to have a closer look at him. All I have to do is go and lunch at the Filet de Sole, on Place des Victoires, where he is supposed to hold his meetings."

"Be careful."

"I know."

He went through the inspectors' room to give some instructions. Lapointe had just come back.

"What about the cigars?"

"It's curious that it should have been a woman who noticed this detail. The owner of the bistrot can't say whether the man smoked a pipe, a cigar, or a cigarette, though he stayed at his bar for more than a quarter of an hour. Mademoiselle Blanche's concierge is quite definite."

"He smoked a cigar?"

"No—a cigarette. He threw the butt on the stairs and stepped on it."

It was one o'clock when Maigret walked into the famous restaurant on Place des Victoires, with a certain apprehension, for as a humble employee it was hardly prudent to measure oneself against a Mascoulin. He had nothing specific against him except a brief note which the deputy could explain in hundreds of different ways. Here, Mascoulin was on his own ground. Maigret was clearly the intruder, and the headwaiter watched him come in without rushing to welcome him.

"Do you have a table?"

"For how many?"

"I'm alone."

Most of the tables were occupied, and there was a continuous hum of conversation, accompanied by the noise of knives and forks and the clinking of glasses. The headwaiter looked around and moved toward a table smaller than the others, tucked behind a door. Finally, in response to a sign, the cloakroom attendant came to take Maigret's coat and hat.

Three other tables were free, but if the Superintendent had indicated them, he would probably have been told that they were reserved, which was quite possible. He had to wait for a long time before his order was taken and had every opportunity of observing everyone in the room.

The restaurant was popular among top-echelon people, and at luncheon they were mostly men, bankers, well-known lawyers, journalists, and politicians, all belonging more or less to the same circle and making signs of recognition to one another. Some had recognized the Superintendent, and he was probably talked of in hushed tones at several tables.

Joseph Mascoulin was sitting in the right-hand corner, on a seat against the wall, in the company of Maître Pinard, a lawyer almost as famous as the deputy for the ferocity of his speeches. A third companion had his back to Maigret; he was a middle-aged man with narrow shoulders and sparse gray hair swept over the bald skull. It was only when he turned sideways that the Superintendent recognized him to be Sauvegrain, the brother-in-law and associate of Nicoud, whose photograph he had seen in the papers.

Mascoulin, who was eating a steak, had already spotted Maigret and stared at him as if there was no one else of any interest in the room. At first his eyes lit up with curiosity, which was followed with a faint gleam of irony, and now he seemed to be waiting with amusement for the Superintendent's next move. The latter had at last given his order; he added to it half a bottle of Pouilly and went on smoking his pipe in little puffs, returning the deputy's stare with unconcern. The difference between them was that, as always in such moments, Maigret's eyes appeared vacant. One had the impression that the object he was staring at was as neutral, as uninteresting as a blank wall and that he was thinking of nothing beyond the sole Dieppoise he had just ordered.

He was far from knowing the complete history of Nicoud and his enterprise. Popular belief claimed that Sauvegrain, the brother-in-law, who until he married Nicoud's sister about ten years ago was only an obscure contractor, participated in the business only in name. He had an office on Avenue de la République, not far from Nicoud. It was a vast, luxurious office, but Sauvegrain spent his days in it waiting for visitors of small consequence who were sent to him to pass away the time.

Mascoulin must have had his reasons for accepting

him openly at his table. Was Maître Pinard there because he looked after Sauvegrain's interests?

A newspaper editor stopped at Maigret's table on his way out and shook his hand.

"On the job?" he asked. And as the Superintendent pretended not to understand:

"I don't think I've ever seen you here before."

His eyes turned in Mascoulin's direction.

"I didn't know that Police Headquarters took on that kind of case. Have you found Piquemal?"

"Not yet."

"Still searching for the Calame report?"

This was said in a bantering tone, as though the Calame report had existed only in the imagination of certain people or as though, if it did exist, Maigret would never be able to find it.

"We're searching" was Maigret's evasive reply.

The journalist opened his mouth, then did not say what he was on the point of saying, and walked out with a cordial wave of the hand. In the doorway he just avoided bumping into a newcomer whom Maigret probably would not have noticed had he not had his eyes on the newspaperman.

Just as he was about to push open the second door, the man, in fact, saw the Superintendent through the glass pane and his face expressed a certain alarm. Ordinarily, he would have greeted Maigret, whom he had known for many years. He almost did so, then threw a hesitant glance in Mascoulin's direction and, hoping perhaps that Maigret had not had time to recognize him, made an abrupt rightabout-turn and vanished.

Mascoulin, from his corner, had missed nothing of the scene, but his poker face registered nothing.

What was Maurice Labat doing at the Filet de Sole, and why had he beaten a retreat when he saw Maigret in the restaurant?

For about ten years he had been working in a department on the Rue des Saussaies, and there had even been a time, though a very brief one, during which he was believed to have had an influence on the Minister.

Suddenly it was learned that he had handed in his resignation, then that he had not done so of his own free will, but to avoid some more serious unpleasantness. Since then he had continued to be seen on the fringe of circles which frequented places like the Filet de Sole. He had not, as had many others in the same situation, opened an agency of private investigation. No one knew what his profession was, nor what his resources were. Besides having a wife and children, he had a mistress in an apartment on Rue de Ponthieu, who was twenty years younger than he and must have cost him a pretty penny.

Maigret was neglecting his sole Dieppoise and not paying it the attention it deserved, for the Labat incident had given him plenty to think about.

Was it not natural to assume that the person whom the former policeman had come to see at the Filet de Sole was none other than Mascoulin? Labat was that man in a thousand whom one could entrust with slightly shady jobs, and he must have kept some friends on the Rue des Saussaies. Did he hope, in beating a hasty retreat, that Maigret had not had time to recognize him?

Had Mascoulin, whom the Superintendent was not able to observe at that moment, given him a sign not to come in? If Labat had been about forty, stout, and smoking a cigar, the Superintendent would have been certain that he had discovered the man who had gone to Boulevard Pasteur and Rue Vaneau and who had spirited Piquemal away.

But Labat was barely thirty-six. He was a Corsican and looked like one. Small and slender, he wore high-heeled shoes in order to appear taller and had a brown mustache like two commas. Last but not least, he smoked cigarettes from morning till night, and his fingers were yellow with nicotine. But his appearance nevertheless gave Maigret food for thought, and he reproached himself for being so hypnotized by the Rue des Saussaies. Labat had been one of them but was no longer, and there must have been dozens like him in Paris, of whom Criminal Investigation had got rid for more or less similar reasons. Maigret made a mental note to get hold of a list of these men. He was tempted to telephone Lucas right away and ask him to prepare it. The reason why he decided against it was, strange as it may seem, that he hesitated to cross the room under Mascoulin's mocking eyes. Mascoulin, who had not ordered any dessert, was already at the coffee stage. Maigret did not order any dessert either, only some coffee and brandy, and began to fill his pipe, mentally recapitulating faces that he had known in the Rue des Saussaies. He felt like a man searching for a name that is on the tip of his tongue but which keeps eluding him.

From the moment the stout man had been mentioned, and particularly since a cigar had been brought into the picture, something had been stirring in his memory. He was so wrapped up in his own thoughts that he hardly noticed that Mascoulin had risen and was wiping his lips with his napkin and exchanging a few words with his companions. More precisely he watched him rise, push the table to make way for himself, and finally move quietly across the room toward him, but it was as though all this did not concern him at all.

"May I, Superintendent?" Mascoulin was saying, holding the back of the chair facing Maigret.

His face was serious, with a slight, ironical quiver in the corner of his mouth which might have been only a nervous tic.

For a moment Maigret was confused. He had not expected this. He had never heard Mascoulin's voice, which was grave and had a pleasant quality to it. It was said that it was because of his voice that some women, in spite of his unappealing Grand Inquisitor's face, fought for places in the Chamber when he was expected to speak.

"What a curious coincidence that you should have come here today. I was going to telephone you."

Maigret remained impassive, for he was determined to make Mascoulin's task as difficult as possible, but the deputy did not seem to be at all discountenanced by his silence.

"I've learned only just now that you are working on Piquemal and the Calame report." He spoke in an undertone, because of the other people in the room; they were being watched from several tables.

"Not only have I got important information to pass on to you, but I believe I ought to make an official announcement. Perhaps you would like to send one of your inspectors to the Chamber a little later, to put it on record? Anyone will tell him where to find me."

Maigret remained unperturbed.

"It's about this Piquemal, with whom it happens I was in contact last week."

Maigret had Mascoulin's letter in his pocket and began to understand why the man felt it necessary to speak to him.

"I don't remember which day it was, my secretary handed me one of the many letters that I receive every week and that he has to answer. It was signed Piquemal and gave as address a hotel on Rue Jacob, I have forgotten the name—the name of some provincial town, I think."

Without taking his eyes off Mascoulin's face, Maigret sipped his coffee and went on puffing at his pipe.

"Every day, as you can imagine, I receive hundreds of letters from every type of person: cranks, semi-lunatics, honest men who point out to me some violation of rights or other, and it is my secretary's job—he's a worthy young man in whom I have full confidence—to separate the sheep from the goats."

Why did it cross Maigret's mind, as he was studying the other man's face, that Mascoulin was a homosexual? There had never been the slightest hint of anything like that. If he was, he concealed it carefully. It occurred to the Superintendent that it might explain certain traits in his character.

"The Piquemal letter seemed sincere to me, and I'm certain you would have the same impression, if I can find it again, for I shall consider it my duty to send it to you. In it he told me that he was the only man in Paris to know the whereabouts of the Calame report and to be able to lay hands on it. He added that he addressed himself to me rather than to an official body because he knew that too many people were interested in hushing up the story and that I was the only one who inspired him with confidence. I apologize for repeating these words. I sent him a note on the off chance, giving him an appointment."

Very calm, Maigret pulled his notebook out of his pocket and took from it the letter with the Chamber of Deputies letterhead, which he merely showed, without handing it across the table in spite of Mascoulin's movement to snatch it.

"Is it this note?"

"I believe so. I seem to recognize my own handwriting."

He did not ask how it had come to be in Maigret's possession, avoided showing any surprise, and said:

"I see you know all about it. I met him at the Brasserie du Croissant, which is not far from the printers and where I keep some of my appointments in the evening. He seemed to me a little too excited, too cranky for my taste. I let him speak."

"He told you that he had the report?"

"Not in so many words. Men like him never behave as simply as that. They need an atmosphere of conspiracy. He told me he was working in the School of Engineering, that he had been Professor Calame's assistant, and that he thought he knew where to find the report

Calame had written on the subject of the Clairfond sanatorium. The conversation didn't last more than ten minutes, because I had some proofs to read."

"After that Piquemal brought you the report?"

"I never saw him again. He suggested bringing it to me on Monday or Tuesday, at the latest on Wednesday. I replied that I didn't want to touch it—you can understand my reasons. That report is sheer dynamite, as we have seen today."

"To whom did you advise him to hand it?"

"To his chief."

"You mean the Director of the School of Engineering?"

"I don't think I was so precise. I may have mentioned the Ministry which naturally came to mind."

"Did he try to telephone you?"

"Not that I know of."

"Nor to see you?"

"If he did, he didn't succeed, for as I told you before, I had no news of him except from the papers. It seems that he followed my advice, going somewhat beyond it, for he went straight to the Minister. As soon as I heard about his disappearance I told myself I must let you know about the incident. Now it's done. Considering the possible repercussions it might have, I prefer to make a statement and have it properly recorded. So, this afternoon . . . if . . ."

There was no way out. Maigret would have to send someone to him to take his statement. The inspector would find Mascoulin surrounded by his colleagues and journalists. Was it not an excellent way of accusing Auguste Point?

"Thank you," was all he said. "I'll give the necessary instructions."

Mascoulin seemed taken aback, as though he had expected something different. Had he imagined that the Superintendent would put embarrassing questions to him or in one way or another show his disbelief?

"I'm only doing my duty. If I'd known how things were going to turn out I'd have told you about it before. . . ."

He seemed to be playing a part all the time, almost, one would have sworn, without attempting to conceal it. He appeared to be saying: "I've been smarter than you. Try to find an answer to that one!" Had Maigret made a mistake in coming here? Certainly, from one point of view, because he had nothing to win—on the contrary, he had everything to lose, in measuring himself against a man as powerful and as crafty as Mascoulin.

The deputy stood up and held out his hand. The Superintendent was suddenly reminded of Point and his story about dirty hands. Without weighing the pros and cons, he picked up his cup of coffee, which was empty, and put it to his lips, thus ignoring the hand that was offered to him.

A shadow seemed to flicker in the deputy's eyes. The quiver in the corner of his mouth, far from disappearing, became more accentuated.

But he only murmured:

"Good-by, Monsieur Maigret."

Did he intentionally stress the "Monsieur"? It seemed to Maigret he did. If so it was a barely disguised threat, for it meant that Maigret was not to be allowed to enjoy his title of Superintendent for very long.

He followed him with his eyes as he went back to his table and bent over his companions, then called in an absent-minded way:

"Waiter, check, please."

At least a dozen persons who, in one capacity or another, played an important part in the life of the country had their eyes fixed on him.

Maigret must have downed his brandy without noticing it; as he went out, he was surprised to find the flavor of it still in his mouth.

7

It was not the first time he had made this kind of entrance, more as a friend than as a boss. He opened the door of the inspectors' room and, pushing his hat to the back of his head, went and sat on a corner of a table. He emptied his pipe on the floor by knocking it against his heel and then filled another one. He was watching them, one after the other, as they busied themselves about their different jobs, somewhat like a father who comes home in the evening, pleased to be among his brood and counting them up.

Some time elapsed before he growled:

"Lapointe, my boy, I guess you're going to have your picture in the papers."

Lapointe raised his head, trying not to blush, his eyes expressing incredulity. In fact, all of them, with the exception of Maigret, who was much too used to it, were secretly delighted when newspapers published their photographs. But every time it happened, they never failed to protest:

"With such publicity, it'll be easy now to work under cover without anyone noticing us!"

The others were listening too. If Maigret had come to speak to Lapointe in the main office, it meant that what he had to say to him was addressed to them all.

"You're going to provide yourself with a shorthand notebook and go to the Chamber. You won't have any trouble finding the deputy Mascoulin, I'm sure, and I'll be surprised if you don't find him surrounded by people. He will make a statement to you, which you will carefully take down. Then you'll come here and type it and leave it on my desk."

The afternoon papers were bursting from his pockets, with the photograph of Auguste Point and his own on the front page. He had hardly looked at them. He knew almost exactly what was being said.

"Is that all?" asked Lapointe, who had gone to get his overcoat and hat from the closet.

"For the moment."

Maigret remained where he was, smoking dreamily:

"Listen, my children . . ."

The inspectors raised their heads.

"I want you to think of some of the Rue des Saussaies men, who were either dismissed or obliged to resign. . . ."

"You mean recently?" asked Lucas.

"It doesn't matter when. Let's say during the last ten years."

Torrence exclaimed:

"There must be a whole bunch of them!"

"Well, give me some names, then."

"Baudelin. The one who is investigator for an insurance company now."

Maigret tried to recall Baudelin, a tall, pale young man who probably left Criminal Investigation not because of dishonesty or indiscreet behavior, but because he devoted more energy and skill to pleading ill-health than doing his job.

"Anyone else?"

"Falconet."

He was over fifty; he had been asked to retire early because he had started to drink and had become unreliable.

"Anyone else?"

"Little Valencourt."

"Too small."

Contrary to what they had expected at the beginning, they could think of only a few names, and each time, after conjuring up the man's appearance, Maigret shook his head.

"It doesn't really fit. I'm looking for a stoutish man, someone like myself."

"Fischer."

There was a general burst of laughter, because the man weighed at least two hundred pounds.

"Thanks!" growled Maigret.

He stayed with them for a while and finally he sighed and got to his feet.

"Lucas, would you please telephone the Rue des Saussaies and ask for Catroux?"

Now that he was interested only in inspectors who

had left Criminal Investigation, he no longer felt that he was asking his friend to betray his colleagues. Catroux, who had worked for twenty years on the Rue des Saussaies, would be better placed than his own men to answer his question. There was a feeling in the air that the Superintendent was on to something, that he was working on an idea; it was still vague, perhaps not yet quite clear even to him. His sham gruffness, his eyes that stared at people without seeing them, were a sign that he knew now in which direction to search.

He kept trying to remember a name which he had had on the tip of his tongue a moment ago. Lucas was telephoning, talking in a warm, familiar way to the man on the other end of the line, who must have been a friend.

"Catroux's not there, Chief."

"You're not going to tell me that he's on some job at the other end of France?"

"No, he's ill."

"In the hospital?"

"No, at home."

"Did you ask for his address?"

"No, I thought you had it."

It is true, they were good friends, Catroux and he. Nevertheless they had never been in each other's homes. Maigret could only remember leaving his colleague one day at his door, at the far end of Boulevard des Batignolles, on the left, and he remembered a restaurant to the right of the door.

"Has Piquemal's photo appeared in the papers?"

"Yes, on the second page."

"No one has telephoned about it?"

"Not yet."

He went to his office, opened a few letters, standing up, took Torrence some papers that concerned him, and finally went down to the yard, where he hesitated over using one of the Police Department cars. Finally he took a taxi. Though his visit to Catroux was quite innocent, he considered it more prudent not to keep a car from the Quai des Orfèvres waiting at the door.

At first he mistook the house, for there were now two restaurants at fifty yards' distance from one another. He asked the concierge:

"Monsieur Catroux?"

"On the second floor, to the right. The elevator is being repaired."

He rang the bell. He did not remember Madame Catroux, who opened the door to him and who, by contrast, recognized him at once.

"Come in, Monsieur Maigret."

"Is your husband in bed?"

"No, he's in an armchair. It's only a severe case of flu. Usually he has one at the beginning of every winter. This time it caught up with him at the end."

On the walls were pictures of two children, a boy and a girl, at every age. Not only were both now married, but photographs of grandchildren were beginning to increase the collection.

"Maigret?" Catroux's delighted voice called out before the Superintendent had reached the door of the room where he was sitting.

It was not a real living room, but a large room where one felt the greater part of the life of the house was lived. Catroux, wrapped in a thick dressing gown, was seated near the window, newspapers in his lap, more of them on a chair nearby, a cup of tisane on a small table. He held a cigarette in his hand.

"You're allowed to smoke?"

"Sh-sh. . . . Don't side with my wife. Only a few puffs now and again, to take away the taste."

He was hoarse and his eyes were feverish.

"Take off your overcoat. It must be very hot in here. My wife insists that I've got to sweat. Do sit down."

"May I give you a drink, Monsieur Maigret?" the wife asked.

She looked like an old woman, and the Superintendent was surprised by that. He and Catroux were about the same age. It seemed to Maigret that his own wife looked much younger.

"Of course, Isabelle. Whatever he says—go and bring the bottle of old calvados."

There was an embarrassed silence between the two men. Catroux obviously knew that his colleague had not come to inquire about his health, and he perhaps expected even more embarrassing questions than Maigret had in mind.

"Don't worry, old fellow. I have no wish to get you into any trouble."

At this point, the other man glanced at the front page of the newspaper as though saying: "This is what it's about, isn't it?"

Maigret waited for his glass of calvados.

"And what about me?" his friend protested.

"You're not supposed to have any."

"The doctor said nothing about that."

"I don't need a doctor to tell me what to do."

"Just a drop, for the taste of it!"

She gave him a drop and disappeared discreetly, as Madame Maigret would have done.

"I have an idea in the back of my mind," admitted Maigret. "My inspectors and I tried to draw up a list of people who have worked with you and been bounced."

Catroux was looking at the paper, trying to link what Maigret was saying with what he had just read.

"Bounced, why?"

"Never mind why. You know what I mean. It happens with us too but less often because there are fewer of us."

Catroux gave a teasing smile.

"Is that what you think?"

"Perhaps also because we are not involved with so many things. Let's put it this way, the temptation is less strong. We racked our brains just now, but we could think of only a few names."

"Which names?"

"Baudelin, Falconet, Valencourt, Fischer. . . ."

"Is that all?"

"More or less. I thought it would be better to come and see you. They are not what I'm looking for. I want the men who have gone to the bad."

"Someone like Labat?"

Was it not strange that Catroux should have mentioned this particular name? He might almost have done it on purpose, as a way of slipping Maigret some information.

"I did think of him. He's probably mixed up in it all right. But he's not the one I'm looking for."

"You've got a specific name in mind?"

"A name and a face. I started off with a description,

and from the beginning it reminded me of someone. Since then . . ."

"What is the description? We'll get on more quickly than if I give you a whole list. Especially since I haven't got all the names in my head, either."

"First of all, people took him to be a policeman right away."

"This could apply to plenty of people."

"Middle-aged. Somewhat stouter than average but not as stout as I am."

Catroux seemed to be estimating the size of his friend.

"Either I'm greatly mistaken, or he is making inquiries on his own behalf or for someone else."

"A private investigator?"

"Perhaps. He won't necessarily have put his name on an office door, or advertised in the papers."

"There are plenty of them, including lots of old, perfectly decent men, who have reached the age limit and then opened an agency. Louis Canange, for example. And Cadet, who was my chief."

"We have some of those, too. I mean the other kind."

"What else is in your description?"

"He smokes cigars."

Immediately Maigret realized that his friend had thought of a name. His forehead wrinkled. He looked distressed.

"It means something to you?"

"Yes."

"Who?"

"A bad one."

"That's what I'm looking for."

"A bad one in a small way, but dangerous."

"Why?"

"Firstly, that kind of person is always dangerous. Furthermore, he's believed to do some politicians' dirty work."

"It fits perfectly."

"You think he's mixed up in this business?"

"If he answers to the description I've given you, if he smokes cigars and meddles in politics there's every chance he's my man. You don't want to . . ."

Suddenly Maigret could see a face before him, a rather large face, bags under the eyes, thick lips pulled out of shape by cigar smoking.

"Wait. . . . It's coming back to me. It's . . ."

But he still could not get the name.

"Benoît," prompted Catroux, "Eugène Benoît. He's opened a small private office on Boulevard Saint-Martin, on the ground floor over a watchmaker. His name is on the glass door. I believe the door is more often locked than open; the whole staff of the agency consists of himself."

It was the man whom the Superintendent had been trying to remember for the past twenty-four hours.

"I don't suppose it would be easy to get his photo?"

Catroux thought a moment before replying.

"It depends on the date when he left the service. It was . . ."

He made some calculations under his breath and then called out:

"Isabelle!"

Isabelle was not far away and came running.

"Look on the lower shelf of the bookcase for a register of the Criminal Investigation Department. There's only one, dating back several years. It contains two or three hundred photos."

His wife found it at once and he turned the pages, pointed his finger to his own portrait, and found what he was searching for at the back of the book.

"There you are! There he is. He's a few years younger there, but he hasn't changed much. He's always been stout, as far as I can remember."

Maigret recognized him too, for he had in fact met him in the past.

"Do you mind if I cut out the photo?"

"Of course not. Isabelle, bring some scissors."

Maigret slipped the bit of glossy paper into his pocket and got to his feet.

"You're in a hurry?"

"Yes, rather. And I'm sure you'd rather we didn't pursue this any further."

The other man understood what he meant. Until Maigret knew exactly what Criminal Investigation was doing it was healthier for Catroux that his colleague should tell him as little as possible about it.

"You aren't afraid?"

"Not really.

"And you believe that Point . . . ?"

"I'm convinced that they're trying to make a scapegoat of him."

"Another drink?"

"No, thank you. Get well soon."

Madame Catroux saw him to the door, and when he left the house he took another taxi and told the driver to go to Rue Vaneau. He was just trying out his luck.

He knocked at the concierge's lodge. She recognized him.

"Forgive me for bothering you again. I would like you to look carefully at a photograph and tell me if this was the man who went up to Mademoiselle Blanche's apartment. Take your time."

It was not necessary. After a moment's hesitation, she shook her head.

"Definitely not."

"You're certain?"

"Quite certain."

"Even if the photo dates back a few years and the man has changed?"

"Even if he was wearing a false beard, I'd swear that's not the man."

He looked at her out of the corner of his eye. For a moment the idea occurred to him that this was a prepared reply. But no, she looked perfectly sincere.

"Thank you," he sighed, slipping the photograph back into his pocket.

It was a blow. He had been almost certain that he was on the right track, and it had come to nothing at the first testing.

His taxi was waiting, and because it was nearby he told the driver to go to Rue Jacob, and there he walked into the bistrot where Piquemal had always had his breakfast. There was hardly anyone there at this time of day.

"Would you look at this photo?" he asked the owner.

He almost avoided looking at him, fearing what the reply would be.

"That's him, absolutely. Only he seemed to me a little older than that."

"That's the man who came up to Piquemal and left your place with him?"

"That's him."

"You are quite certain?"

"Absolutely."

"Thank you."

"Won't you have a drink?"

"Not now, thanks. I'll be coming back."

This changed everything. Until now Maigret had assumed that the same man had visited different places: Mademoiselle Blanche's apartment, Piquemal's little bar, the Hôtel du Berry, the professor's widow, and Boulevard Pasteur. Suddenly it turned out that there were at least two men.

His next visit was to Madame Calame, whom he found reading the papers.

"I hope you'll find my husband's report. I can understand now why he was so worried in his last years. I've always had such a horror of these filthy politics."

She studied him with suspicion, thinking perhaps to herself that it was because of these "filthy politics" that he had come to see her.

"What is it you want, today?"

He handed her the photograph. She examined it carefully, then raised her head in surprise.

"Ought I to be able to recognize him?"

"Not necessarily. I was wondering if he was the man who visited you two or three days after Piquemal."

"I've never seen him."

"You couldn't be mistaken about that?"

"No. It could be the same type of person, but I'm certain it's not the man who came here."

"Thank you."

"What happened to Piquemal? Do you think they killed him?"

"Why?"

"I don't know. If they are desperate to hush up the report my husband wrote, then they've got to get rid of everyone who knows about it."

"They didn't get rid of your husband."

This reply clearly put her out. She felt obliged to protect her husband's memory.

"My husband knew nothing about politics. He was a scientist. He was doing his duty when he wrote the report and when he passed it on to the proper quarters."

"I'm quite sure that he was doing his duty."

He decided to go before she started discussing the matter in greater depth. The taxi driver gave him a sour look.

"Where now?"

"To the Hôtel du Berry."

He found a couple of journalists there, looking for information on Piquemal. They rushed up to Maigret, but he shook his head.

"I've nothing to tell you, boys. Just a routine check. I promise you that . . ."

"D'you hope to find Piquemal alive?"

So that's what they were thinking, too?

He left them in the hallway and went to show the photograph to the hotel proprietor.

"What am I supposed to do with this?"

"Tell me if he's the man who came to talk to you about Piquemal."

"Which one?"

"Not my inspector, who hired a room, but the other one."

"No."

He was quite definite. So far, Benoît was the man who had left the bar with Piquemal, but he had not been seen anywhere else.

"Thank you."

He jumped into the taxi.

"Drive on . . ."

Only when they had started and he had got rid of the journalists did he give the Boulevard Pasteur address. He did not stop at the lodge but went straight up to the third floor. No one answered the bell, so he had to go down again.

"Madame Gaudry is not at home?"

"She went out half an hour ago with her son."

"Do you know when she'll be back?"

"She wasn't wearing her hat. She must be shopping in the neighborhood. I don't think she'll be long."

Rather than wait on the sidewalk, he went to the bar where he had been in the morning, and telephoned Headquarters. Lucas answered from the inspectors' room.

"Anything new?"

"Two telephone calls about Piquemal. The first from a taxi driver who believes he drove him yesterday to the Gare du Nord. The other from a movie cashier who thinks she sold him a ticket yesterday evening. I'm going to check."

"Is Lapointe back?"

"He came in a few minutes ago. He hasn't started to type yet."

"Put him on, will you?"

And to Lapointe:

"Well? Any photographers?"

"Yes, they were there, Chief, clicking away the whole time while Mascoulin was speaking."

"Where did he see you?"

"In the Columns Room. It was just like Saint-Lazare station! The ushers had to hold the crowd back to give us room to breathe!"

"Was his private secretary there?"

"I don't know. I wouldn't recognize him. We never met."

"Is it long?"

"It'll run to about three typed pages. The reporters took shorthand notes the same time as I did."

So Mascoulin's statement would be in the last edition of the evening papers.

"He insisted that I take it to him to sign."

"What did you say?"

"That it wasn't my affair. That I would wait for your orders."

"Do you know if there is a night session at the Chamber?"

"I don't think so. I heard them say that it would be over by five o'clock."

"Type it out and wait for me."

Madame Gaudry was not back yet. He paced the sidewalk for a while and saw her arrive, carrying a shopping bag of provisions, her son trotting at her side. She recognized him.

"Is it me you want to see?"

"Just for a moment."

"Come upstairs. I've just been doing my marketing."

"Maybe it isn't worth while coming up."

The boy was pulling at her sleeve, asking:

"Who is it? Why does he want to talk to you?"

"Be quiet. He just wants some information from me."

"What information?"

Maigret had pulled the photograph out of his pocket.

"Do you recognize him?"

She managed to free herself, bent over the piece of glossy paper, and answered quite spontaneously:

"Yes, that's him."

Now he was sure that Eugène Benoît, the man with the cigar, had been in two places: first on Boulevard Pasteur, where he had probably stolen the Calame report, then in the Rue Jacob bar, where he had gone up to Piquemal, leaving with him in the direction opposite to the School of Engineering.

"Have you found him?" asked Madame Gaudry.

"Not yet. It won't take us long, though."

He hailed another taxi to take him to Boulevard Saint-Martin, regretting that he had not taken a Police car, for now he would have to explain his expenses to the accountant.

The house was an old one. The lower part of the mezzanine windows was of frosted glass, carrying in black letters the inscription:

BENOIT AGENCY

Investigations of all kinds

On both sides of the doorway name plates announced an artificial flowers business, a Swedish masseuse, and other professions, some of them of the more unexpected kind. The stairs on the left were dark and dirty. The name of Benoît appeared again on an enamel plate attached to a door. He knocked, knowing beforehand that there would be no reply, for there was a heap of printed matter pushed under the door. After waiting for a moment, to ease his conscience, he went down and found the lodge in the courtyard. There was no concierge in it, only a shoemaker who used it as a workshop.

"Is it long since you have seen Monsieur Benoît?"

"I haven't seen him today, if that's what you want to know."

"And yesterday?"

"I don't know. I don't think so. I didn't notice."

"And the day before?"

"Nor that day either."

He had a mocking air about him, and Maigret pushed his badge under the man's nose.

"I've told you all I know. I don't mean any harm. The tenants' business doesn't concern me."

"D'you know his home address?"

"It would be in the ledger."

He rose reluctantly and went to get a filthy register from a cupboard in the kitchen, and turned the pages with fingers black with pitch.

"The last I have is the Hôtel Beaumarchais on Boulevard Beaumarchais."

It was not far away, and Maigret walked there.

"He moved three weeks ago," they told him. "He only stayed here for two months."

This time he was directed to a rather shady boarding-house on Rue Saint-Denis, in front of which stood an enormously fat girl who opened her mouth to say something, then recognized him at the last moment and shrugged her shoulders.

"He has room 19. He's not at home."

"Did he spend the night here?"

"Emma! Did you do Monsieur Benoît's room this morning?"

A head came over the banisters of the first floor.

"Who's asking for him?"

"Never mind who it is. Tell me."

"No. He didn't spend the night here."

"And the night before?"

"No."

Maigret asked for the room key. The girl who had answered from the first floor followed him to the third, on the pretext that she was showing him the way. As the doors were numbered, he had no need of her at all. But he asked her a few questions.

"Does he live alone?"

"Are you asking me if he sleeps alone?"

"Yes."

"Quite often."

"Has he got a regular girl friend?"

"He has plenty of them."

"What kind?"

"The kind that is willing to come here."

"Are they often the same ones?"

"I have seen the same face two or three times."

"Does he pick them up in the street?"

"I'm not there to see."

"He hasn't been here for two days?"

"Two or three days. I'm not quite sure."

"Do men sometimes come and see him?"

"If you mean what I think you mean, he's not that type, and the hotel isn't, either. There's one of those kind of places farther down the street."

The room revealed little to Maigret. It was a typical room for a place of that sort, with a brass bed, an old chest of drawers, a dilapidated armchair, and hot and cold running water. The drawers contained some underclothes, a half-empty box of cigars, a broken watch, fish-hooks of different sizes in a cellophane bag, but no interesting papers. In a suitcase with expanding sides he found only shoes and dirty shirts.

"Does he often stay away overnight?"

"More often than not. And every Saturday he goes to the country until Monday."

This time Maigret drove back to the Quai des Orfèvres, where Lapointe had long since finished typing Mascoulin's statement.

"Get me the Chamber on the phone and find out if the deputies are still in session."

"Am I to say you want to speak to him?"

"No. Don't mention either me or the police."

When he turned to Lucas, the latter shook his head.

"There was one other call after the first two. They've been checked. Torrence is still on it. There was nothing in them."

"Nothing to do with Piquemal?"

"No. The taxi driver was quite certain it was him, but his client was traced back to his own house and it wasn't Piquemal."

There would be new leads, especially in tomorrow's mail.

"The session in the Chamber finished half an hour ago," Lapointe announced. "It was just a vote on . . ."

"I don't care what the vote was on."

He knew that Mascoulin lived on Rue d'Antin, two steps away from the Opéra.

"Are you busy at the moment?"

"No, nothing important."

"In that case come with me and bring the statement along."

Maigret never took the wheel. He had tried several times, after Headquarters had been provided with a number of small black cars, and he had forgotten he was driving, he was so deep in thought. Two or three times he had remembered his brakes only at the last moment, and now he had no wish to repeat the experience.

"Do we take a car?"

"Yes."

It was as if to make amends to the accounting department for all his taxis that afternoon.

"Do you know the number on Rue d'Antin?"

"No. It's the oldest house."

The house looked respectable, old, but well kept up.

Maigret and his companion stopped in front of the lodge, which was like the living room of a lower-middle-class family and smelled of floor polish and plush.

"Monsieur Mascoulin."

"Do you have an appointment?"

Maigret took a chance and said yes. The woman in black looked at him, then glanced at the front page of the paper and back at him again.

"I suppose I have to let you go up, Monsieur Maigret. It's on the first floor to the left."

"Has he been living here long?"

"It'll be eleven years in December."

"Does his secretary live with him?"

She gave a little laugh.

"Certainly not."

He got the impression that she had guessed what he was driving at.

"They work late at night?"

"Often. Almost always. I think Monsieur Mascoulin must be the busiest man in Paris, to go by all the mail he gets here and at the Chamber."

Maigret was tempted to show her Benoît's photograph and ask if she had seen him before, but she would probably talk about it to her tenant, and Maigret was not prepared to show his hand just yet.

"Are you connected with him by a private line?"

"How do you know that?"

It was not difficult to guess because beside the ordinary telephone there was another, lighter one, attached to the wall. Mascoulin took no chances. And she would warn him of Maigret's arrival as soon as he and Lapointe were on the stairs. It did not matter. He could have prevented it by leaving Lapointe in the lodge.

First, no one answered the bell, but a little later Mascoulin himself opened the door, without even bothering to show that he was surprised.

"I thought you would come in person and that you would choose to come here. Come in."

The floor was littered with newspapers, periodicals, parliamentary debates, reports. There were more of them in a room that served as a living room and that was about as attractive as a dentist's waiting room. Obviously, Mascoulin was interested in neither luxury nor comfort.

"I expect you would like to see my study?"

There was something insulting in his irony, in his manner of pretending to guess his visitors' intentions, but the Superintendent retained his composure.

"I'm not one of your fans coming to ask for your autograph," was all he replied.

"Will you come this way?"

They went through a padded double door and found themselves in a spacious study, both windows of which overlooked the street. Green filing cabinets covered two of the walls. There were lawbooks that one finds in every lawyer's room everywhere, and finally here too the floor was littered with newspapers and files, as many as in any Ministry.

"May I introduce René Falk, my secretary?"

René Falk was not more than twenty-five, fair-haired, frail, with a strangely childish, petulant expression.

"Pleased to meet you," he said in a low voice, looking at Maigret in much the same manner as Mademoiselle Blanche had looked at him the first time she met him. Like Mademoiselle Blanche, he too was no doubt fanatically devoted to his employer and regarded every stranger as an enemy.

"You've brought the statement? With several copies, I presume?"

"I've brought three copies; two of them are for you to sign, as you wished, and the third for your files or for whatever purpose you choose."

Mascoulin took the documents and passed one to René Falk, who began to read it at the same time as his boss.

Sitting at his desk, he took a pen, added a comma here and there, deleted a word, and then murmured, turning to Lapointe:

"I hope you don't mind?"

When he came to the last line, he signed, transferred the corrections to the second copy, and signed it also.

Maigret held out his hand, but Mascoulin did not give him the pages. Nor did he transfer the corrections to the third copy.

"Correct?" he asked his secretary.

"Yes, I think so."

"Now have them photostated."

He looked maliciously in Maigret's direction.

"A man who has as many enemies as I have cannot afford to be careless," he said. "Particularly when there are so many people determined to keep a certain document from the public eye."

Falk opened a door and left it open behind him so that a small room was visible, no doubt previously a kitchen or bathroom. A machine was standing on a white wooden table. The secretary pressed some buttons. The machine gave a humming sound as he pushed in the pages one after the other. Maigret, who knew the system, but who had rarely seen a machine of this kind in a private house, followed the operation with apparent indifference.

"Marvelous invention, isn't it?" Mascoulin said, his lips curving in the same ugly smile. "A carbon copy can be questioned. But you can't argue with a photostat."

A faint smile flickered across Maigret's face and the deputy noticed it.

"What's on your mind?"

"I was just wondering if, out of all the people who have had the Calame report in their possession recently, one of them had had the idea of having it photostated."

It was not inadvertently that Mascoulin had let him see the machine. Falk could easily have disappeared with the documents for a moment, without the Superintendent's knowing what he was going to do in the next room.

The pages came out through a slot and the secretary spread them out, still damp, on the table.

"It would be a nasty trick to play on anyone interested in hushing the affair up, wouldn't it?" Mascoulin said with a leer. Maigret looked at him in silence, his expression perfectly neutral, and at the same time at its most ominous.

"Yes, a nasty trick," he repeated. And an imperceptible cold shudder ran down his spine.

8

It was half past six when the two men reached Boulevard Saint-Germain, and the yard of the Ministry was empty. As Maigret and Lapointe crossed it in the direction of the stairs leading to the Minister, a voice sounded behind them.

"Hi! You two, over there! Where are you going?"

The guard had not seen them come in. They stood still, turning to him in the middle of the yard, and he limped up to them, glanced at the badge Maigret showed him, then looked at his face.

"I beg your pardon. I saw your picture in the paper a moment ago."

"Good for you! Now you are here, can you tell me . . ." It had become a habit, this taking the photograph out of his brief case. "Have you seen this face before?"

The man, anxious not to blunder a second time, examined it carefully, after putting on steel-framed spectacles with thick lenses. He was not saying yes or no. Before committing himself he would have liked to ask what it was all about, but he did not dare.

"He's a little older now, isn't he?"

"Yes, a few years older."

"He has a black two-seater, an old model?"

"It's possible."

"Then it's probably the fellow I caught parking in the yard in the space reserved for the Ministry cars."

"When was that?"

"Can't remember the day. At the beginning of the week."

"Did he give his name?"

"He just shrugged his shoulders and went and parked his car at the other end."

"Did he go up the big staircase?"

"Yes."

"Try to remember the day, while we're upstairs."

In the waiting room on the first floor, the usher was still at his post reading the newspapers. Maigret showed him the photograph, too.

"When might he have been here?" he asked.

"Around the beginning of the week."

"I wasn't here. My wife died and I had to take four days off. We'll have to ask Joseph. He'll be here next week. Am I to announce you to His Excellency?"

A moment later Auguste Point himself opened the door of his study. He seemed tired but calm. He let Maigret and Lapointe in without asking any questions. His secretary, Mademoiselle Blanche, and his private parliamentary secretary were both in the study. The

Ministry did not yet supply its servants with radios, and the one on the table, a small portable, no doubt belonged to Point—the three people in the study had probably been listening to it when the usher interrupted them.

". . . the session was a brief one, devoted exclusively to current affairs, but the lobbies were at fever pitch all afternoon. All kinds of conflicting rumors have been circulating. A sensational announcement is expected on Monday, but it is still not known . . ."

"Turn it off!" said Point to his secretary.

Fleury made as if to move toward one of the doors but Maigret held him back.

"You needn't go, Monsieur Fleury. Nor you, Mademoiselle."

Point was watching him anxiously, for it was difficult to guess what the Superintendent had come for. On the other hand he looked like a man who has got an idea and is so obsessed by it that he forgets everything else.

He appeared to be mentally drawing a plan of the office. He studied the walls, the doors.

"Will you allow me, Your Excellency, to put two or three questions to your colleagues?"

He turned first to Fleury.

"I imagine you were in your office during Piquemal's visit?"

"I knew nothing of . . ."

"I don't doubt it. But *now* you know. Where were you at that time?"

He pointed to a double door that was half open.

"Is that your office?"

"Yes."

The Superintendent went and had a look at it.

"Were you alone?"

"I couldn't really tell you that. I'm not often alone for any length of time. Visitors come and go the whole day. The Minister sees some of them, the more important ones, and the rest I see myself."

Maigret opened a door that led directly from the parliamentary secretary's office to the waiting room.

"Do they come in this way?"

"Usually, yes. Except those the Minister sees first and then brings to me for one reason or another."

The telephone rang. Point and Mademoiselle Blanche exchanged glances. Mademoiselle Blanche lifted the receiver.

"No. His Excellency is not in. . . ."

She listened, a fixed expression in her eyes. She, too, looked exhausted.

"The same thing?" asked Point, when she had put down the receiver.

She nodded, keeping her eyes down.

"He said his son was . . ."

"Please . . ."

He turned to Maigret.

"The telephone has never stopped since midday. I've taken several of the calls myself. Most of them say the same thing: 'If you try to hush up the Clairfond affair, we'll get your hide!' There are different versions of it, some more polite than others. Some even give their names, often the parents of the children who died in the disaster. One woman was terribly distressed, and yelled at me over the phone: 'You're not going to cover up for the murderers, are you? If you haven't destroyed the report, show it, so that the whole of France can know . . .' "

He had dark shadows under his eyes, from lack of sleep, and his face was gray.

"The President of my electoral committee in La Roche, a man who was my father's friend and knew me when I was in short pants, called me a moment ago, almost directly after my statement went on the air. He didn't accuse me, but I could feel he had his doubts. He sounded quite sad. He simply said: 'They don't understand out here, son. They knew your parents and they believe they know you. Even if you have to scuttle the lot of them, you've got to tell everything you know.' "

"You'll be telling it soon," replied Maigret.

Point lifted his head abruptly, not sure whether he had heard correctly, and asked, hesitantly:

"You really think so?"

"I'm quite certain now."

Fleury was leaning against a chest at the other side of the office. Maigret gave the Minister Benoît's photograph; he looked at it, puzzled.

"Who is this?"

"You don't know him?"

"I don't seem to recall his face."

"He hasn't been to see you, recently?"

"If he'd been to see me, his name would be in the register in the waiting room."

"Would you show me your office, Mademoiselle Blanche?"

Fleury was unable from a distance to see the photograph, and Maigret noticed that he was biting his nails, as if it was a lifelong habit.

The door of Mademoiselle Blanche's office, adjoining that of the parliamentary secretary, was small and narrow.

"This is where you went when Piquemal arrived and your employer asked you to leave him alone with him?"

Very tense, she nodded her head in affirmation.

"You closed the door behind you?"

She nodded again.

"You can hear what is being said in the next room?"

"If I put my ear to the door and if the conversation is loud enough, I probably would."

"You didn't do that?"

"No."

"Does it ever happen that you do?"

She preferred not to answer. Perhaps she might listen, for example, if Point were visited by a woman she considered attractive or dangerous?

"Do you know this man?"

She was waiting for this, for she had glanced at the photograph when the Minister was looking at it.

"Yes."

"Where did you see him?"

She spoke in a low voice, so that the others should not hear her.

"In the office near mine."

She pointed with her finger to the wall that separated them from Fleury's office.

"When?"

"On the day of Piquemal's visit."

"After it?"

"No. Before."

"Was he sitting or standing?"

"He was sitting, with his hat on, and a cigar in his mouth. I didn't like the way he was looking at me."

"Did you see him again?"

"Yes. Afterward."

"Are you saying that he was still there when Piquemal left, and that he stayed in that office all the time the visit lasted?"

"I think so. He was there, before and after. You believe that . . . ?"

She probably wanted to talk to him about Fleury, but all he said was:

"Sh. . . . Come."

When he returned to the large office, Point looked at him with reproach, as though upset that Maigret should have been badgering his secretary.

"Will you need your parliamentary secretary this evening, Your Excellency?"

"No. Why?"

"Because I would like to have a talk with him."

"Here?"

"Preferably in my office. Will it be inconvenient for you to come with us, Mr. Fleury?"

"I have a dinner engagement, but if it's a matter of urgency . . ."

"Will you call and say you'll be busy?"

Fleury did as he was told. Leaving the door of his office open, he telephoned Fouquet's.

"Bob? It's Fleury speaking. Has Jacqueline arrived? . . . Not yet? . . . You're sure? . . . When she comes ask her to start without me. . . . Yes. . . . I probably won't come for dinner. . . . Later, yes. . . . I'll be seeing you. . . ."

Lapointe was watching him out of the corner of his eye. Point, perplexed, was looking at Maigret, obviously longing to ask for an explanation. But the Superintendent appeared not to notice.

"Are you busy tonight, Your Excellency?"

"I was to preside at a banquet, but I called it off before the others could do it first."

"I may possibly telephone to give you some news, probably rather late."

"Even if it's in the middle of the night . . ."

Fleury had reappeared, carrying his coat and hat and looking like a man who is keeping erect through sheer force of habit.

"Ready? Ready, Lapointe?"

They went down the great staircase in silence and walked over to the car which they had left by the sidewalk.

"Get in. . . . To the Quai, Lapointe."

They did not exchange a word on the way. Fleury opened his mouth twice to speak, but thought better of it and bit his nails continuously.

On the dusty stairs Maigret made him go in front and walk first into his office, where he went to close the window.

"You can take off your coat. Make yourself comfortable."

He made a sign to Lapointe, who joined him in the hallway.

"You'll stay with him until I come back. I'll be some time. It's possible that you'll have to be on duty for a part of the night."

Lapointe flushed red.

"You have an appointment?"

"It doesn't matter."

"Can you telephone?"

"Yes."

"If she wants to come and keep you company . . ."

Lapointe shook his head, meaning it wouldn't do.

"Ask for sandwiches and coffee to be sent over from the brasserie. Don't take your eyes off Fleury. Don't let him call anybody. If he asks questions—you know nothing. I want him to stew in his own juice for a while."

It was the classic treatment. Lapointe had taken part in most of the inquiry, but now he was at sea.

"Go and keep him company. Don't forget the sandwiches."

He went into the inspectors' room and found Janvier, not yet gone for the night.

"Have you anything special on tonight?"

"No. My wife . . ."

"She's waiting for you? Can you telephone her?"

He sat down on one of the tables and, lifting the receiver off another telephone, dialed Catroux's number.

"It's Maigret speaking. . . . Forgive me for bothering you again. . . . Something came back to me a moment ago because of some fishhooks I found. Once when I met Benoît, on a Saturday, at the Gare de Lyon, he was going fishing. . . . What did you say? He's a rabid fisherman? Do you know where he usually goes to fish?"

Maigret was now quite confident of what he was doing; he knew he was on the right track, and it seemed that nothing was going to stop him.

". . . What? He has a shack somewhere? Could you find out where? . . . Yes. . . . Now. . . . I'll be waiting near the phone. . . ."

Janvier was still talking to his wife, asking how all the children were, and they all came in turn to wish him good night.

"Good night, Pierrot. . . . Sleep well. . . . Yes, I'll be there when you wake up. Is that you, Monique? Has your little brother been a good boy? . . ."

Maigret waited, with a sigh. When Janvier hung up he said:

"We might have quite an exciting night. Perhaps I'd better call my wife too."

"Shall I dial the number?"

"I have to wait for an important message first."

Catroux had promised to telephone a colleague, another fisherman, who had gone fishing with Benoît at various times.

It was all a matter of luck now. It was possible that the colleague would not be at home. He might be on some job far from Paris. Silence lasted in the office for about ten minutes, and finally Maigret sighed:

"I need a drink!"

At the same moment the telephone rang.

"Catroux?"

"Yes. Do you know Seineport?"

"A little above Corbeil, near a sluice gate." Maigret was remembering an inquiry, long ago . . .

"That's it, it's a small village on the Seine, a favorite place with rod fishermen. Benoît owns a shack near the village. It used to be a guardhouse, very dilapidated; he bought it for a song about ten years ago."

"I'll find it."

"Good luck!"

He did not forget to call his wife, but—alas—he had no children to come and wish him good night over the telephone.

"Ready?"

As he passed the half-opened door of his office he could see that Lapointe had lit the lamp with the green shade and was sitting in Maigret's own chair, his legs crossed, looking tense, his eyes half closed.

"See you soon, boy."

The parliamentary secretary started, got up to ask something, but the Superintendent had already closed the door.

"Do we take the car?"

"Yes. We're going to Seineport, about ten miles away."

"I've been there before with you."

"That's right. Are you hungry?"

"If we have to stay long . . ."

"We'll stop at the Brasserie Dauphine."

The waiter was surprised to see them.

"So I needn't take the sandwiches and beer to your office that Monsieur Lapointe ordered?"

"Yes, please do. But first of all give us something to drink. What will you have, Janvier?"

"I don't know. . . ."

"A Pernod?"

Maigret needed one. Janvier could see it and he had one, too.

"Will you make us a couple of sandwiches each?"

"What would you like?"

"It doesn't matter. Some pâté if you have it."

Maigret seemed to be calm personified.

"We are too used to criminal cases," he muttered to himself, his glass in his hand.

No reply was needed. He was mentally making one himself.

"In a criminal case, there is usually one guilty man or a group of guilty men acting together. In politics it's quite different, and the proof is that there are so many parties in the Chamber."

This idea appeared to amuse him.

"A great many people have an interest in the Calame report, and from different points of view. It's not only the politicians who would be in a mess if the report were published. And not only Arthur Nicoud. There are some for whom possession of the report would procure hard cash and others for whom it would mean power."

There were few customers there that night. The lamps were lit, the air sultry as before a storm.

They ate their sandwiches at Maigret's usual table, and Maigret was reminded of Mascoulin's table at the Filet de Sole. Each had his own table, in different places and in even more different surroundings.

"Some coffee?"

"Yes, please."

"A brandy?"

"No. I'm driving."

Maigret took none either, and a little later they left Paris by the Porte d'Italie and drove along the road to Fontainebleau.

"It's funny to think that if Benoît had smoked a pipe, instead of those stinking cigars, our job would have been infinitely more difficult."

They were going through the suburbs. Soon they had only large trees on both sides of the road and cars with their lights on, going in both directions. Many of them overtook the small black car.

"Shall I step on it?"

"It isn't necessary. Either they are there or . . ."

He knew men of Benoît's type well enough to be able to put himself in their place. Benoît did not have much imagination. He was just a small-time crook, and his small trickeries had not brought him much luck.

He needed women, never mind what kind of women, a loose bohemian life, in places where he could be loud-mouthed and pretend to be a strong man, with, at the end of the week, a day or two of fishing.

"As far as I can remember, there's a small café on the square at Seineport. Stop there and we'll make some inquiries."

They crossed the Seine at Corbeil and followed a road along the river with woods on the other side. Four or five times Janvier had to brake sharply to avoid the rabbits, and every time he growled:

"Get out of the way, you little idiot!"

From time to time a light showed through the darkness; then there was a cluster of street lamps, and the car stopped in front of a café where some men were playing cards.

"Am I to come in, too?"

"If you'd like a drink."

"Not now."

Maigret went in and had a quick drink at the bar.

"D'you know Benoît?"

"The one from the police?"

At Seineport Benoît had not considered it necessary, after so many years, to disclose that he was no longer in Criminal Investigation.

"D'you know where he lives?"

"Did you come from Corbeil?"

"Yes."

"You must have passed him. Did you see a quarry about a mile from here?"

"No."

"At night you can miss it. His house is just opposite, on the other side of the road. If he's there, you'll see a light."

"Thank you."

One of the card players lifted his head.

"He *is* there."

"How d'you know?"

"Because yesterday I sold him a leg of lamb."

"A whole leg for him alone?"

"He doesn't stint himself, it seems to me."

A few minutes later, Janvier, who was driving very slowly, pointed to a spot of light in the wood.

"This must be the quarry."

Maigret looked on the other side of the road and about a hundred yards away, on the riverbank, saw a light in a window.

"You can leave the car here. Let's walk."

There was no moon, but they soon found a thickly overgrown path.

9

They walked silently, single file, unheard by whoever was in the cottage. That part of the riverside must once have belonged to a large estate, and the shack might have been the gamekeeper's lodge.

The grounds were neglected now. A broken-down fence surrounded what used to be a vegetable garden. Through the lighted window Maigret and Janvier could see the beams of the ceiling, whitewashed walls, and a table at which two men were playing cards.

Janvier looked at Maigret, in the dark, as though asking him what they were going to do.

"Stay here," whispered the Superintendent. He himself, however, moved toward the door. It was locked and he knocked on it.

"Who is it?" came a voice from inside.

"Open up, Benoît."

There was a silence, the sound of steps. From his place at the window Janvier could see the former policeman standing by the table. He was hesitating as to what to do, then he pushed his companion into the next room.

"Who is it?" repeated Benoît from the other side of the door.

"Maigret."

Another silence. The bolt was pushed back, the door opened. Benoît looked at Maigret's silhouette, a bewildered expression in his eyes.

"What do you want with me?"

"Just a little chat. Come in, Janvier."

The cards were still on the table.

"All alone?"

Benoît did not answer at once, suspecting that Janvier had been watching at the window.

"You were perhaps playing patience?"

Janvier said, pointing to the door:

"The other one's in there, Chief."

"I thought so. Bring him in."

Piquemal would have found it difficult to run away because the door led to a cesspool without any communication with the outside world.

"What do you want with me? Have you got a warrant?" Benoît blurted out, trying to regain his composure.

"No."

"In that case . . ."

"In that case, nothing! Sit down. And you, Piquemal. I hate talking to men who are standing up."

He fiddled with some cards on the table.

"Were you trying to teach him belote for two players?"

Piquemal had probably never played a game of cards before.

"Are you going to sit down, Benoît?"

"I have nothing to say."

"Very well. In that case, I'll just have to do the talking, won't I?"

There was a bottle of wine on the table and only one glass. Piquemal, who did not play cards, did not drink either, nor did he smoke. Had he ever been to bed with a woman? Probably not. He was looking at Maigret savagely, like an animal at bay.

"Have you been working for Mascoulin for a long time?"

In fact, in this setting, Benoît made a better impression than in Paris, perhaps because he was in his natural element. He had remained the peasant who must have been the braggart of his village, and he had been wrong to leave it to try his luck in Paris. His tricks, his shady practices were those of a peasant at a fair.

To pick up courage, he poured himself some wine and added jestingly:

"And how about you?"

"Thanks. Mascoulin needs people like you, if only to check on the information that comes in to him."

"Go on talking."

"When he received the letter from Piquemal, he realized that it was the opportunity of a lifetime and that he had every chance, if he played his cards well, of keeping a large number of political figures under his thumb."

"That's your opinion."

"That's my opinion."

Maigret was still standing. His hands clasped behind his back, his pipe between his teeth, he paced up and down from the door to the fireplace, stopping from time to time in front of one of the men, while Janvier, sitting on the corner of the table, listened attentively.

"What surprised me most was that having seen Piquemal and having actually had his hands on the report, he should have sent him to the Minister of Public Works."

Benoît smiled knowingly.

"I only understood it just now, when I saw the photostating machine at Mascoulin's place. Shall we take events in their chronological order, Benoît? You can always stop me if I'm wrong.

"Mascoulin receives Piquemal's letter. Being a cautious man, he calls you and tells you to make inquiries. You realize that it is serious, that the fellow is indeed well placed to get hold of the Calame report. At this stage you tell Mascoulin that you know someone quite important in Public Works—the parliamentary private secretary. Where did you meet him?"

"That's none of your business."

"It doesn't matter anyway. He's waiting in my office and we'll be able to settle details like that shortly. Fleury is a sad dog, always short of funds. But he has the advantage of having access to circles where scum like yourself finds the door shut in his face. I dare say he's given you an occasional tip before on some of his friends, in return for a few bank notes."

"Go right on."

"Now perhaps you'd like to come along with me. If

Mascoulin himself takes the report from Piquemal he is practically forced to make it public and to explode the whole scandalous business, for Piquemal is an honest man in his way, a fanatic, whom you would have to kill to silence. To take the report to the Chamber would of course put Mascoulin in the limelight for a time, agreed. But it would be more interesting to hold on to it, and keep in suspense all the people the report compromises. It took me quite a long time to work that one out. I'm not perverted enough to put myself in his shoes. So Piquemal goes to Madame Calame, where he knows, because he's seen it before, that there is a copy of the report. He slips it into his brief case and rushes to Mascoulin, Rue d'Antin. Knowing that he is there, there is no reason for you to follow him, as you know what's going to happen, and you dash to the Ministry of Public Works, where Fleury takes you to his office. Under some pretext or other Mascoulin keeps Piquemal with him while his smooth secretary photographs the report. With all the appearance of an honest man, he then dispatches his visitor to the person it concerns, that is to say, to the Minister. I think that's correct, so far?"

Piquemal was looking intensely at Maigret, deep in his own thoughts, in the grip of a violent emotion.

"You are there, in Fleury's office, when Piquemal hands over the papers. All that you have to do now is to find out, through Fleury, where and when you can get hold of them. In this way, thanks to the honest Mascoulin, the Calame report will be placed at the disposal of the public. But, thanks to you, Auguste Point, the Minister in question, will be unable to present it to the Chamber. So there will be a hero in the story—Mascoulin. There will be a villain, accused of having destroyed the document to save his face, as well as the face of all his colleagues who are compromised—a certain Auguste Point, who has the misfortune of being an honest man and of having refused to shake dirty hands. Quite clever, isn't it?"

Benoît poured himself another glass, which he began to drink slowly, glancing uncertainly at Maigret. He seemed to be asking himself what card it would be in his best interest to play, as he had done at belote.

"That's almost the whole story. Fleury told you that his boss had taken the Calame report to Boulevard Pasteur. You didn't dare to go there at night, because of the concierge, but the next morning you waited until she had gone to do her marketing. Did Mascoulin burn the report?"

"It's not my business."

"Whether he burned it or not, it doesn't matter, because he had the photostat. That was quite enough to keep quite a number of people under his thumb."

It was mistake, Maigret realized afterward, to insist on Mascoulin's power. If he hadn't, would Benoît have acted differently? Probably not, but it was a risk to take.

"The bomb exploded, as foreseen. Other people were searching for the document for different reasons, among others a certain Tabard, who had been the first to remember Calame's part in the affair and to allude to it in his paper. You know that wretched Tabard, don't you? It wouldn't have been power he would have got from the report, but hard cash. Labat, who worked for him, probably prowled around Madame Calame's place.

Did he see Piquemal leave her house? I don't know and it's possible that we'll never know. But it doesn't really matter. Anyhow, Labat sent one of his men to the widow, then another to the Minister's secretary. . . . You remind me, all of you, of a lot of crabs crawling and scratching about in a basket. Others, too, more officially, asked themselves what exactly had happened and tried to find out."

He was referring to the Rue des Saussaies. Once the President of the Council had been informed, it was natural that a more or less discreet inquiry should be made by the Criminal Investigation Department. From then on the situation became almost comical. Three different groups had chased the report, each for its own reasons.

"The weak spot was Piquemal, because it was difficult to tell whether he might not talk under interrogation. Was it you, I wonder, who had the bright idea of bringing him here, or was it Mascoulin? You're not prepared to say. Well, it doesn't matter. Anyway, the point was to withdraw him from circulation for a while. I don't know how you went about it or what story you had to tell him. You've noticed no doubt that I'm not questioning him. He'll talk when he sees fit to do so, when he realizes that he's been nothing but a pawn in the hands of two crooks, a big one and a small one."

Piquemal gave a start, but remained silent.

"Well, that's about it, for now. We're outside the Seine department, as you will no doubt point out to me, and I'm exceeding my authority."

He waited for a moment, then murmured:

"Put the handcuffs on him, Janvier."

Benoît's first reaction was to resist, and he was twice as strong as Janvier. Then, after a moment's reflection, he held out his wrists and chuckled to himself.

"It'll cost you something, the two of you. You realize I haven't said a word."

"Not a word. Will you come with us, too, Piquemal, if you please? You're perfectly free, but I don't suppose you want to stay here?"

As they went out Maigret turned back to switch off the light.

"You've got the key?" he asked. "It would be better to lock the door, for it'll be some time before you're fishing here again."

They climbed into the small car and drove in silence.

At the Quai des Orfèvres they found Fleury still sitting in his chair. He jumped when he saw the former inspector of the Rue des Saussaies in the doorway.

"I needn't introduce you," growled Maigret.

It was half past eleven. The building was deserted, with lights only in two of the offices.

"Get me the Ministry."

Lapointe dialed a number.

"Superintendent Maigret wants to speak to you."

"Forgive me for disturbing you, Your Excellency. You weren't in bed, I hope? You're with your wife and daughter? . . . I've got news, yes. . . . It's important. . . . Tomorrow you'll be able to give the Chamber the name of the man who burgled your apartment on Boulevard Pasteur and took away the Calame report. . . . Not right away, no. . . . In an hour, perhaps, or maybe two. . . . Yes, wait for me if you prefer. . . . I can't guarantee it won't be the morning."

It lasted three hours. For Maigret and his men it was an old, familiar routine. They all stayed together for a long time in the Superintendent's office, Maigret doing the talking and stopping now and then in front of one man or the other.

"Just as you please, boys. I've all the time in the world, you know. You take one of them, Janvier. . . . This one, I think. . . ."

He pointed to Piquemal, who so far had not opened his mouth.

"And you can get busy with Monsieur Fleury, Lapointe."

Thus, in each office, there were two men, one questioning, the other trying to keep silent. It was a test of endurance. Sometimes Lapointe or Janvier would appear in the doorway, make a sign to the Superintendent, and then they would both walk out into the hallway and talk in undertones.

"I have at least three witnesses to confirm my story," Maigret said to Benoît. "Among them, and this is the most important one, a tenant from Boulevard Pasteur who saw you enter Point's apartment. You still refuse to talk?"

What Benoît finally said was characteristic of him:

"What would you do in my place?"

"If I were as much of a scoundrel as to be in your place, I'd make a clean breast of it."

"No."

"Why?"

"You know very well why."

He couldn't move against Mascoulin! Benoît knew well that Mascoulin would always manage to wriggle out of the mess somehow, and God alone knew what would happen to his accomplice.

"Don't forget that he's the one who has the report."

"So?"

"So nothing. I'm keeping my mouth shut. They'll charge me with burgling the apartment on Boulevard Pasteur. How much will I get for that?"

"About two years."

"As for Piquemal, he came with me of his own accord. I never threatened him. So I didn't kidnap him."

Maigret realized he would get nothing further from him.

"You admit you went to Boulevard Pasteur?"

"I'll admit it if I can't help it. That's all."

And a few minutes later it became impossible for him to help it. Fleury had collapsed and Lapointe came to tell his chief.

"He knew nothing about Mascoulin, had no idea until tonight who Benoît was working for. He couldn't refuse to help Benoît because of certain transactions they had had in the past."

"Did you get him to sign a statement?"

"I'm doing it now."

If Piquemal was an idealist, he was an idealist who had gone wrong. He continued in fact to keep silent. Was he relying on the possibility that this would bring him something from Mascoulin?

At half past three Maigret, leaving Janvier and Lapointe with the three men, drove in a taxi to Boulevard Saint-Germain, where there was a light in a second-floor window. Point had given orders that Maigret should be taken immediately to his apartment.

Maigret found the family in the small living room where he had been received before.

"Do you have the document?"

"No. But the man who stole it from Boulevard Pasteur is in my office and has confessed."

"Who is it?"

"An old Criminal Investigation man who took the wrong turn and works for anyone who will pay him."

"Whom was he working for this time?"

"Mascoulin."

"In that case," began Point, his expression darkening again.

"Mascoulin will say nothing, he'll be quite content to wait, and then when the need arises he can put pressure on anyone who is compromised. He'll let Benoît take the blame. As for Fleury . . ."

"Fleury?"

Maigret nodded.

"He's a pitiable wretch. He found himself in such a position that he couldn't refuse. . . ."

"I told you so," interrupted Madame Point.

"I know. I didn't believe it."

"You're not made for political life. When all this is over I hope you . . ."

"The essential thing," Maigret was saying, "is to establish that you didn't destroy the Calame report and that it was stolen from you as you said."

"Will they believe me?"

"Benoît will confess."

"Will he say whom he did it for?"

"No."

"And Fleury won't, either?"

"Fleury didn't know."

"So that in the end . . ." A burden had been lifted from his heart, but there was nothing to celebrate in it. Maigret had undoubtedly saved his reputation, but Point had lost the game. Unless at the last moment Benoît decided to tell the whole truth, and that was very unlikely, the real winner was Mascoulin. Mascoulin himself was so confident of his victory that even before Maigret had come to the end of his inquiry he had purposely shown him the photostat. It had been a warning. It simply meant "To whom it may concern—watch out!"

Anyone who had anything to fear from the publication of the report, whether it was Arthur Nicoud, still in Brussels, a politician, or whoever, knew now that Mascoulin had only to lift a finger, and they would be finished, their careers ruined.

There was a long silence in the room; Maigret was not feeling very proud of himself.

"In a few months, when all this is forgotten, I'll hand in my resignation and go back to La Roche-sur-Yon," murmured Point, staring at the carpet.

"Is that a promise?" his wife pleaded.

"It is."

There were no reservations to her happiness, for her husband meant more to her than anything else in the world.

"May I call Alain?" Anne-Marie asked.

"At this hour?"

"Don't you think it's worth waking him up for?"

"If you wish. . . ."

She, too, did not quite realize what the situation meant.

"Would you like a drink?" Point said, looking almost timidly at Maigret. Their eyes met. Once again the Superintendent had the impression that the man beside him resembled him like a brother. Both looked at each other with the same sadness of defeat, their shoulders hunched.

The drink was merely an excuse to sit down together for a moment. The young woman was telephoning.

"Yes. . . . It's all finished. . . . We mustn't talk about it yet. . . . We must let Papa surprise them all, when he goes up to the rostrum in the Chamber."

What were the two men to say to one another?

"Your health!"

"Yours, Your Excellency!"

Madame Point had left the room and Anne-Marie soon followed her.

"I'm going to bed," murmured Maigret, as he stood up. "You need it even more than I do."

Point held out his hand, clumsily, as if it were not an everyday gesture, but the expression of a feeling that he was too shy to admit.

"Thanks, Maigret."

"I did what I could."

"I know."

They walked to the door.

"I too refused to shake his hand. . . ."

And on the landing, before turning his back on his host:

"He'll get what's coming to him, one of these days."